The Dominance of Global Corporations

Other Books in the Global Viewpoints Series

Biodiversity and Conservation
Chemical and Biological Warfare
Citizenship in the 21st Century
Climate Change and Population Displacement
Gender Diversity in Government
Global Health
Human Trafficking
Modern Conflict and Diplomacy
National Identity
Reproductive Rights
The Rise of Authoritarianism

The Dominance of Global Corporations

Avery Elizabeth Hurt, Book Editor

Published in 2020 by Greenhaven Publishing, LLC
353 3rd Avenue, Suite 255, New York, NY 10010

Copyright © 2020 by Greenhaven Publishing, LLC

First Edition

All rights reserved. No part of this book may be reproduced in any form without permission in writing from the publisher, except by a reviewer.

Articles in Greenhaven Publishing anthologies are often edited for length to meet page requirements. In addition, original titles of these works are changed to clearly present the main thesis and to explicitly indicate the author's opinion. Every effort is made to ensure that Greenhaven Publishing accurately reflects the original intent of the authors. Every effort has been made to trace the owners of the copyrighted material.

Cover image: Andrey Tolkachev/Shutterstock.com, © Can Stock Photo/ Volokhatiuk (clouds), © Tsiumpa/Dreamstime.com (earth)

Map: frees/Shutterstock.com

Library of Congress Cataloging-in-Publication Data

Names: Hurt, Avery Elizabeth, editor.
Title: The dominance of global corporations / Avery Elizabeth Hurt, book editor.
Description: First edition. | New York : Greenhaven Publishing, 2020. | Series: Global viewpoints | Includes bibliographical references and index. | Audience: Grades 9–12.
Identifiers: LCCN 2019022822 | ISBN 9781534506442 (library binding) | ISBN 9781534506435 (paperback)
Subjects: LCSH: Corporate power—Juvenile literature. | International business enterprises—Political aspects—Juvenile literature.
Classification: LCC HD2731 .D66 2020 | DDC 306.3/4—dc23
LC record available at https://lccn.loc.gov/2019022822

Manufactured in the United States of America

Website: http://greenhavenpublishing.com

Contents

Foreword   11

Introduction   14

Chapter 1: Corporate Dominance Around the World

1. How the Rise of Corporate Power Changed the World   19
   Anup Shah

   The history of the corporation goes back much further than most people realize. The author discusses corporations and how those entities have been viewed from the sixteenth century in Europe to their present global presence.

2. Small and Medium-Sized Businesses Need Less Regulation Than Large Ones   29
   EurActive

   This viewpoint argues that big corporations are good for nations' economies but that small companies may need a little help getting there.

3. In **Tanzania** Investment by China Brings Hope and Questions   33
   Nick Van Mead

   China's increased investment in Africa is discussed in this viewpoint, in which the author explores how Chinese investment could affect African nations.

4. In **Africa**, the Country's Colonial History Affects Its Development   39
   Ewout Frankema

   By taking a look at the history of European colonization in Africa, this viewpoint points out that African nations need to be mindful of their colonial history as they plan for development in the twenty-first century.

5. In **Brazil** an Election Shows That True Power Lies with Corporations, Not Nations 46
   Gary Younge
   This author takes a look at what happens to democracy when global power is in the hands of multinational corporations rather than democratic states.

6. In **China** and the **United States** a Trade War Poses Risks 51
   Charles Hankla
   In discussing the potential risks of a trade war between the United States and China, the author illustrates how global economics affects global politics.

Periodical and Internet Sources Bibliography 57

Chapter 2: Causes and Effects of Global Corporate Dominance

1. Globalization Is Not Living Up to Its Promise 59
   Gail Tverberg
   The author of this viewpoint focuses on the negative aspects of globalization, noting twelve particular examples of how globalization causes environmental, economic, and social harm.

2. Emerging Multinationals Are Embracing Social Responsibility 69
   Wharton School of the University of Pennsylvania
   This article from the business analysis journal of the Wharton School describes how several multinational companies are embracing social responsibility—and explains what's in it for them.

3. Globalization Has Changed the Rules of the Game 76
   Milan Babic, Eelke Heemskerk, and Jan Fichtner
   This viewpoint, from a group of scholars in the Netherlands, examines the potential risks of a world in which corporations share power with nations.

4. In the **United States** a Free Media Is Essential to Democracy, but Corporate Media Really Is "the Enemy of the People" 80
   Paul Street
   Previous viewpoints have primarily discussed multinationals that manufacture and/or sell goods. Here, the author examines the democracy-inhibiting effect of corporate media.

5. The Rise of Global Corporate Power Is Increasing Inequality 91
   Sarah Anderson and John Cavanagh
   The authors present and analyze data showing that the world's economic activity is concentrated in only 200 global corporations and examine the consequences of that consolidation.

6. In the **United Kingdom** Recent Decisions on Parent Company Liability Cases Show the Need for Law Reform 97
   William Meade
   Through their global activities, UK companies are often involved in human rights and environmental abuses. At the present time, there is no statutory regime in the UK for dealing with alleged violations of human rights by corporate actors.

Periodical and Internet Sources Bibliography 103

Chapter 3: Corporate Dominance and Democracy

1. Who Runs the World? 105
   David Smith
   This chapter opens with a viewpoint that takes a historical look at the balance of power between governments and corporations.

2. In the **United States** Corporate Capture Threatens Democratic Government 112
   Liz Kennedy
   The author explains the dangers of letting corporations take control of government away from the people.

3. Citizens Must Work to Contain and Shape Corporate Power   **119**
   K. Sabeel Rahman
   The author discusses two scholarly works about the legal history of corporate control of government and institutions.

4. The Rise of Corporate Power Was the Fall of Democracy   **128**
   Richard Moser
   The author argues that corporate power killed democracy forty years ago. Nothing short of an overthrow of corporate power will restore democracy, he writes.

5. Democracy Is Good for Business   **135**
   Freedom House
   Where previous viewpoints have stressed the damage big business can do to democracy, this viewpoint argues that a strong democracy is in the interest of corporations.

Periodical and Internet Sources Bibliography   **139**

Chapter 4: The Future of a World Dominated by Global Corporations

1. Just 90 Companies Caused Two-Thirds of Man-Made Global Warming Emissions   **141**
   Suzanne Goldenberg
   This viewpoint takes a look at the role of multinational corporations in the most serious crisis of the twenty-first century: global warming.

2. After Paris, Businesses Not Governments Are Leading the Climate Change Fight   **146**
   Daphne Leprince-Ringuet
   Though multinational corporations are responsbile for much of the factors that have led to global warning, this viewpoint says that they are doing more than governments are to combat it.

3. Corporations Need a New Strategy for Responding to Climate Change 151
   Rory Sullivan
   The author argues that corporations, while implementing some emissions-reductions strategies, aren't doing enough. They need to take more risks and embrace the opportunities created by climate change.

4. It's Not Too Late to Save Democracy from Corporate Greed 156
   Japheth J. Omojuwa
   Democracy has sold out to big business, this author says, but it's not too late to hold governments accountable.

5. To Reclaim Democracy, Amend the US Constitution 161
   Reclaim the American Dream
   This viewpoint explores the sudden and intense reaction by state and local governments to the US Supreme Court ruling that gave corporations (and unions) the right to spend unlimited sums in support of political candidates.

Periodical and Internet Sources Bibliography 167

For Further Discussion 168
Organizations to Contact 169
Bibliography of Books 173
Index 174

Foreword

> "The problems of all of humanity can only be solved by all of humanity."
> —Swiss author Friedrich Dürrenmatt

Global interdependence has become an undeniable reality. Mass media and technology have increased worldwide access to information and created a society of global citizens. Understanding and navigating this global community is a challenge, requiring a high degree of information literacy and a new level of learning sophistication.

Building on the success of its flagship series, Opposing Viewpoints, Greenhaven Publishing has created the Global Viewpoints series to examine a broad range of current, often controversial topics of worldwide importance from a variety of international perspectives. Providing students and other readers with the information they need to explore global connections and think critically about worldwide implications, each Global Viewpoints volume offers a panoramic view of a topic of widespread significance.

Drugs, famine, immigration—a broad, international treatment is essential to do justice to social, environmental, health, and political issues such as these. Junior high, high school, and early college students, as well as general readers, can all use Global Viewpoints anthologies to discern the complexities relating to each issue. Readers will be able to examine unique national perspectives while, at the same time, appreciating the interconnectedness that global priorities bring to all nations and cultures.

Material in each volume is selected from a diverse range of sources, including journals, magazines, newspapers, nonfiction books, speeches, government documents, pamphlets, organization newsletters, and position papers. Global Viewpoints is truly global, with material drawn primarily from international sources available in English and secondarily from U.S. sources with extensive international coverage.

Features of each volume in the Global Viewpoints series include:

- An **annotated table of contents** that provides a brief summary of each essay in the volume, including the name of the country or area covered in the essay.
- An **introduction** specific to the volume topic.
- A world map to help readers locate the countries or areas covered in the essays.
- For each viewpoint, **an introduction** that contains notes about the author and source of the viewpoint explains why material from the specific country is being presented, summarizes the main points of the viewpoint, and offers three **guided reading questions** to aid in understanding and comprehension.
- **For further discussion** questions that promote critical thinking by asking the reader to compare and contrast aspects of the viewpoints or draw conclusions about perspectives and arguments.
- A worldwide list of **organizations to contact** for readers seeking additional information.
- A **periodical bibliography** for each chapter and a **bibliography of books** on the volume topic to aid in further research.
- A comprehensive **subject index** to offer access to people, places, events, and subjects cited in the text.

Global Viewpoints is designed for a broad spectrum of readers who want to learn more about current events, history, political science, government, international relations, economics, environmental science, world cultures, and sociology— students doing research for class assignments or debates, teachers and faculty seeking to supplement course materials, and others wanting to understand current issues better. By presenting how people in various countries perceive the root causes, current consequences, and proposed solutions to worldwide challenges, Global Viewpoints volumes offer readers opportunities to enhance their global awareness and their knowledge of cultures worldwide.

Introduction

> *"People are starting to recognize that the dreams of collective prosperity promised by democracy are being turned into nightmares for the majority, and monumental wealth for the privileged ruling class and their allies."*
>
> —*Japheth J. Omojuwa, World Economic Forum, August 19, 2016*

During their long history, corporations have done both good and ill. The purpose of establishing corporations was to limit the liability of the people involved in a business enterprise. The people who provided money for the company—the shareholders—would not be held responsible for the debts of the corporation. They could not lose more than their investment.

A corporation was also considered a "person" in that it had legal standing to sue or be sued, make contracts, and own property. These provisions—particularly the limited liability—were important for entrepreneurship. People would be much more likely to invest in new enterprises if they knew any potential losses were limited.

It's hard to fathom now, but corporations weren't always for-profit entities. The first corporations, established in early-modern Europe, were non-profit organizations operating by royal charter and designed to build hospitals, universities, and contribute to the public good in other ways. Their responsibilities were clearly outlined in their charters and their operations were supervised by the government of the country in which they were chartered.

Introduction

A bit later, corporations were set up as trading companies. They were given monopolies over a specific type of good or a particular region. The East India Company was granted a charter by Queen Elizabeth of England in 1600 and was the first commercial corporation. It was a joint-stock company—money to operate the venture was raised by selling shares in the company—and thus much more like modern corporations than previous charters had been.

The East India Company made fortunes for its investors by trading with India. The East India Company was far more than a business, though. In order to protect their posts from marauders, the company hired its own armies, eventually maintaining an army far larger than that of Britain itself. Soon, the East India Company had become the de facto government of India. However, the enterprise was so riddled with corruption that the English Parliament stepped in and made some reforms, eventually putting the rule of India under the British Crown.

Trading companies were also active in colonizing the New World. The Virginia Company and the Plymouth Company, for example, were major players in establishing colonies in what is now the United States. One of the motivations for the American Revolution was resentment about the monopoly of trade by British corporations. The government of the brand new United States used a system similar to the pre-1600s arrangement in Europe. Corporations were charted for a specific purpose—to build roads or bridges, for example—and for a limited period of time. The ability of corporations to take part in profit-making activities was severely limited, and political participation was completely forbidden.

This arrangement didn't last long, though. By the late nineteenth century, corporations had gained tremendous power in the United States. They were creating monopolies and using their power to influence government, prompting then-presidential candidate Rutherford B. Hayes to say that the United States had become "a government of corporations, by corporations and for corporations."

Corporate power has only increased in the twenty-first century, in the United States and around the world. In 2010, the US Supreme Court ruled that there could be no limit to the amount of money corporations could give to political candidates and campaigns, given modern corporations even more influence over the US government and foreign governments.

Today many corporations have become huge entities operating all over the globe with little loyalty to any one nation but, due to their economic power, an outsized influence over most of the world's governments. Of the one hundred largest economies in the world fifty-one are corporations, and the power they wield is enormous.

Critics of global corporations point out that these huge companies are behind many, if not most, of the ills that face the world today. Global warming, economic colonialism, and even the decline in democratic institutions have been put to the account of multinational corporations.

Others point out that corporations must be given some credit for the good they do—spurring innovation, providing jobs, and opening new markets in developing nations.

In *Global Viewpoints: The Dominance of Global Corporations*, viewpoint authors address the various problems created by global corporate dominance and some that offer solutions to those problems.

Introduction

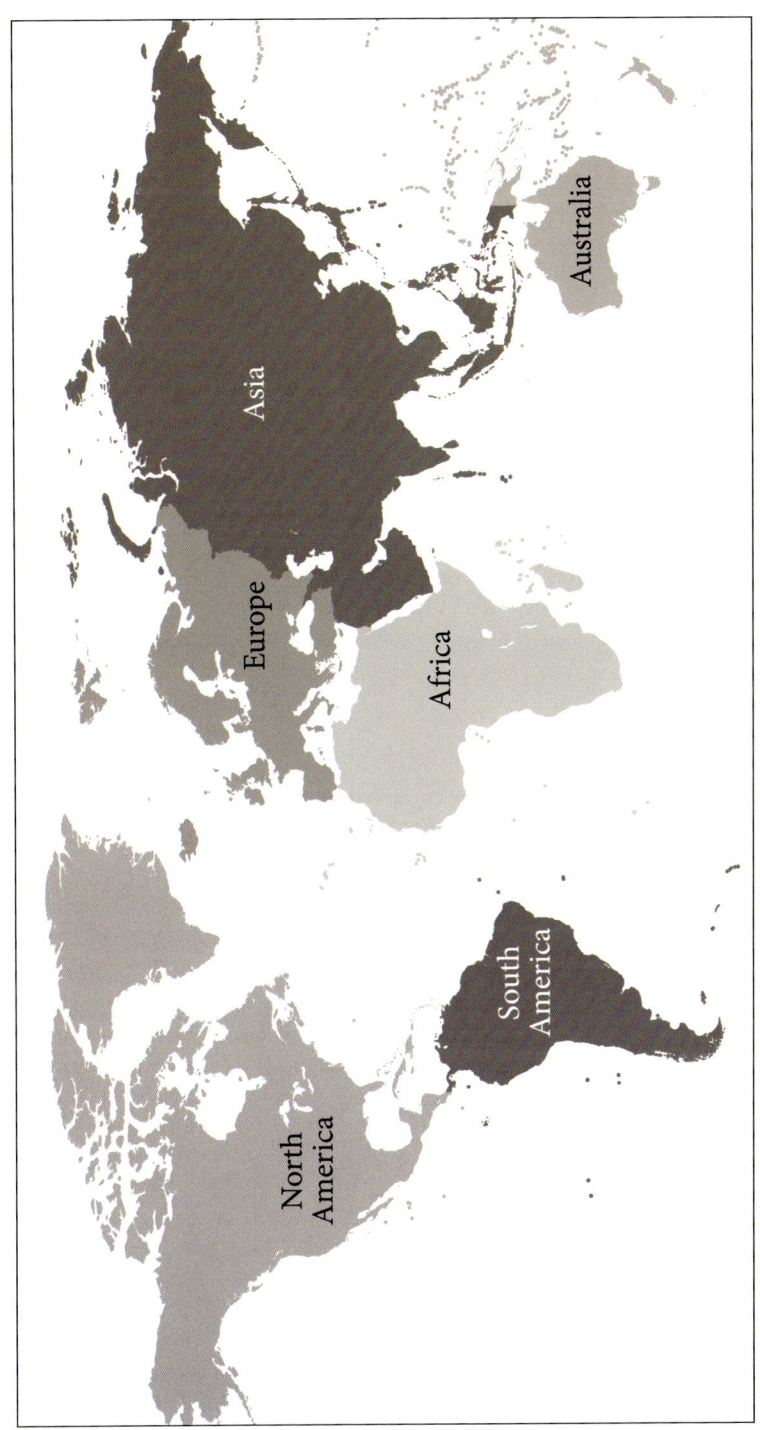

CHAPTER 1

| Corporate Dominance
| Around the World

VIEWPOINT 1

How the Rise of Corporate Power Changed the World

Anup Shah

In the following viewpoint Anup Shaw provides a thorough overview of multinational corporations and their rise in power in recent years, drawing on the work of several other authors. Using quotes from scholars and historical figures, Shah discusses the effects of rights given to corporations and the political power these companies have gained. Anup Shah is the editor of the web site Global Issues.

As you read, consider the following questions:

1. What were Abraham Lincoln's concerns about corporations, according to a quote in this viewpoint?
2. How did the Supreme Court ruling in 1886 eventually lead to the interests of corporations being put above the interests of individuals?
3. How, according to this viewpoint, can increased corporate power lead to war?

Today we know that corporations, for good or bad, are major influences on our lives. For example, of the 100 largest economies in the world, 51 are corporations while only 49 are countries, based on a comparison of corporate sales and country GDPs. In this era of globalization, marginalized people are becoming especially angry at the motives of multinational

"The Rise of Corporations," by Anup Shah, Global Issues, December 5, 2002. http://www.globalissues.org/article/234/the-rise-of-corporations Reprinted by permission.

corporations, and corporate-led globalization is being met with increasing protest and resistance. How did corporations ever get such power in the first place?

[The section is a very broad and high-level overview of the history of corporations. It largely summarizes from the works of people like J.W. Smith, author of World's Wasted Wealth II (Institute for Economic Democracy, 1994) and Economic Democracy; Political Struggle of the 21st Century (M.E. Sharpe, 2000); Giovanni Arrighi, The Long Twentieth Century (Verso Press, 1994 reprinted 2000); Richard Robbins, Global Problems and the Culture of Capitalism (Allyn and Bacon, 1999). Of course, while I do recommend these sources, many, many other sources out there offer similar perspectives and insights.]

The Rise of the Corporation

Corporations, as we tend to think of them, have been around for a few centuries, the earliest of which were chartered around the sixteenth century in places like England, Holland etc. Technically speaking, a corporation is what Robbins describes as a social invention of the state (Robbins: p.98). That is, a state grants a corporate charter, permitting private financial resources being used for public purposes. As Arrighi points out, this initial creation of private finance and merchants, etc was to aid in the expansion of a state to which it belonged, and as Arrighi and Smith detail, served to expand colonial and imperial interests to start with, as well as help in war efforts between empires.

The advantage of having a corporation over being an individual investing in trade voyages etc, was that an individual's debts could be inherited by descendants (and hence, one could be jailed for debts of other family members, for example). A corporate charter however, was limited in its risks, to just the amount that was invested. A right not accorded to individuals. (Robbins: p.98)

Corporations had therefore the potential, from the onset, to become very powerful. Even Abraham Lincoln recognized this:

Corporate Dominance Around the World

> I see in the near future a crisis approaching that unnerves me and causes me to tremble for the safety of my country. ... corporations have been enthroned and an era of corruption in high places will follow, and the money power of the country will endeavor to prolong its reign by working upon the prejudices of the people until all wealth is aggregated in a few hands and the Republic is destroyed.
>
> —U.S. President Abraham Lincoln, Nov. 21, 1864 (letter to Col. William F. Elkins) Ref: The Lincoln Encyclopedia, Archer H. Shaw (Macmillan, 1950, NY)

Adam Smith, in his famous book the Wealth of Nations, the bible of capitalism, was also critical of some aspects of corporate activity. He saw corporations as working to evade the laws of the market, trying to interfere with prices and controlling trade etc.

The Rights of the Corporation

As corporations did manage to increase their wealth and therefore political power, laws that initially tried to manage them were further relaxed. As Arrighi mentions throughout his book, corporations would benefit from the State's war-making activities, further increasing their wealth and influence.

Yet, it was claiming of a corporation to be an individual in the United States in the 1800s, and claiming the same rights as a person that helped to provide for large expansion of corporate capitalism:

> [A U.S.] Supreme Court ruling in 1886 ... arguably set the stage for the full-scale development of the culture of capitalism, by handing to corporations the right to use their economic power in a way they never had before. **Relying on the Fourteenth Amendment, added to the Constitution in 1868 to protect the rights of freed slaves, the Court ruled that a private corporation is a natural person under the U.S. Constitution, and consequently has the same rights and protection extended to persons by the Bill of Rights, including the right to free speech.** Thus corporations were given the same rights to influence the government in their own interests as were extended to individual citizens, paving

the way for corporations to use their wealth to dominate public thought and discourse. The debates in the United States in the 1990s over campaign finance reform, in which corporate bodies can donate millions of dollars to political candidates stem from this ruling although rarely if ever is that mentioned. Thus, corporations, as persons, were free to lobby legislatures, use the mass media, establish educational institutions such as many business schools founded by corporate leaders in the early twentieth century, found charitable organizations to convince the public of their lofty intent, and in general construct an image that they believed would be in their best interests. All of this in the interest of free speech.

—Richard Robbins, Global Problems and the Culture of Capitalism, (Allyn and Bacon, 1999), p.100 (Bold Emphasis Added)

As Robbins further points out, from this ability to influence, corporate libertarianism emerged, which placed the rights and freedoms of corporations above that of individuals. This influence also led to cultural and economic ideologies known by numerous names such as neoliberal, libertarian economics, market capitalism, market liberalism etc.

Some of the guiding principles of this ideology, as Robbins continues, included:

- Sustained economic growth as the way to human progress
- Free markets without government interference would be the most efficient and socially optimal allocation of resources
- Economic globalization would be beneficial to everyone
- Privatization removes inefficiencies of public sector
- Governments should mainly function to provide the infrastructure to advance the rule of law with respect to property rights and contracts.

However, the assumptions behind these principles are questionable as much as the principles themselves. These assumptions, and how neoliberal ideology has developed into today's free trade globalization is further discussed at http://www.globalissues.org/issue/38/free-trade-and-globalization.

The Rise of Corporate Influence

From this right of the corporation, how has it affected the rights of others? Corporations in and of themselves may not be a bad thing. They can be engines of positive change. But, especially when they become excessively large, and concentrated in terms of ownership of an industry and in wealth, they can also be engines for negative change, as seems to have happened. There is of course, the common concern about the drive for profit as the end goal sometimes contradicting the social good, even though it is claimed that the invisible hand ensures the drive for profit is also good for society. Sometimes this has surely been the case. But other times, it has not.

There is much recognized and unrecognized corporate influence in our lives. Indeed, much of western culture and increasingly, around the world, consumerism is expanding.

Corporate influence can reach various parts of societies through various means, which many other entities don't have the ability to do, as they lack the financial resources that corporations have:

- Influence on general populations via advertising and control and influence in the mainstream media.
- Influence on public policy and over governments, as hinted to above. This can range from financing large parts of elections, to creating corporate-funded think tanks and citizen groups, to support from very influential political bodies such as the Trilateral Commission, the Council on Foreign Relations and the Bilderberg group, etc.
- Influence on international institutions, such as the World Trade Organization, as well as international economic and political agreements.

> ## The Responsibilities of Multinationals
>
> Multinational companies (MNCs) are responsible to host countries for their actions there. If they have a presence in the U.S.—as most multinationals do— they are also responsible under U.S. law for their actions even if they were conducted abroad. Further complicating matters, MNCs are also subject to international law. A clear policy of best practices and a corporate support structure are required for the sake of clarity and compliance.
>
> ### Competing Laws
>
> MNCs have a responsibility to obey the laws of each host country, international laws and those of countries with a record of legal intervention in areas such as human rights. Fulfilling this responsibility can be tricky because laws in one country are often incompatible with those in another. That difficulty has increased as international non-governmental organizations (NGOs) have begun pursuing legal remedies in one country for alleged violations elsewhere.
>
> ### Areas of Concern
>
> Some legal issues, such as human rights and employment practices, have been particularly troublesome. For example, U.S. financial company JPMorgan Chase was accused of corruption by the Department of Justice for hiring the sons and daughters of prominent Chinese government officials. The circumstances, as reported in The New York Times, suggested

Thom Hartmann, a writer and reporter, describes at length how corporations co-opted the use of human rights, in his book Unequal Protection: The Rise of Corporate Dominance and the Theft of Human Rights (Rodale Press, October 2002). It details the 1886 ruling also mentioned above on this page. With kind permission, a table contrasting implications before and after that ruling is reproduced here, from a summary page on the web site for the book:

Hartmann actually goes further saying that the ruling never happened:

> that company executives in China may have wandered into the problem naively, believing they were engaging in a common hiring practice in China. U.S. investigators then began probing similar practices by five more Wall Street firms doing business in China.
>
> ## Problem Awareness
>
> A guidance paper from Pinsent Masons, a U.K. law firm with an extensive international practice, suggests that MNCs should address potential problem areas sooner rather than later. Legal departments can conduct preventive research to identify which areas may cause trouble, promote corporate awareness of those problems and suggest solutions before legal issues arise and the courts intervene.
>
> ## Policy Information
>
> Best practices can also arise from an awareness of a company's culture and of what kinds of policies have worked in the past. They may also arise from position papers, in-service education programs or the wisdom of senior legal staff with experience abroad. Countries and NGOs can also help MNCs by informing them of best legal practice in specific countries from an international perspective. The International Law Office, for example, distributes its "Code of Best Practice for Corporate Governance" for Nigeria to global counsel.
>
> *"Legal Practices for Multinational Companies," by Patrick Gleeson, Ph. D., Hearst Newspapers, LLC.*

the Supreme Court ruled no such thing in 1886. The "corporations are persons" ruling was a fiction created by the court's reporter. He simply wrote the words into the headnote of the decision. The words contradict what the court actually said. There is, in fact, in the US National Archives a note by the Supreme Court Chief Justice of the time explicitly informing the reporter that the court had not ruled on corporate personhood in the Santa Clara case.

—Thom Hartmann, Dinosaur War, The Ecologist, December/January 2002 Issue

But since then, either way, the influence and power of large corporations has increased and is an undeniable facet of the "global

The Dominance of Global Corporations

	Before 1886: When Only Humans Had Rights	After 1886: After the Corporate Theft of Human Rights
Rights and Privileges	Only humans were "endowed by their creator with certain inalienable rights" and those human rights included the right to free speech, the right to privacy, the right to silence in the face of accusation, and the right to live free of discrimination or slavery.	While to this day unions, churches, governments, and small unincorporated businesses do not have human rights (but only privileges humans give them), corporations alone have moved into the category with humans as claiming rights instead of just privileges.
Politics	In many states, it was a felony for corporations to give money to politicians, political parties, or try to influence elections: "They can't vote, so what are they doing involved in politics?!"	Corporations claimed the human right of free speech, expanded that to mean the unlimited right to put corporate money into politics, and have thus taken control of our major political parties and politicians
Business	States and local communities had laws to protect and nurture entrepreneurs and local businesses, and to keep out companies that had been convicted of crimes.	Multi-state corporations claimed such laws were "discrimination" under the 14th Amendment (passed to free the slaves) and got such laws struck down; local communities can no longer stop a predatory corporation.
War	Government, elected by and for "We, The People," made decisions about how armies would be equipped and, based on the will of the general populace, if and when we would go to war. Prior to WWII there were no permanent military manufacturing companies of significant size.	Military contractors grew to enormous size as a result of WWII and a permanent arms industry came into being, what Dwight Eisenhower called "the military/industrial complex." It now lobbies government to buy its products and use them in wars around the world.
Regulation	Corporations had to submit to the scrutiny of the representatives of "We, The People," our elected government.	Corporations have claimed 4th Amendment human right to privacy and used it to keep out OSHA, EPA, and to hide crimes.
Purpose	Corporations were chartered for a single purpose, had to also serve the public good, and had fixed/limited life spans.	Corporations lobbied states to change corporate charter laws to eliminate "public good" provisions from charters, to allow multiple purposes, and to exist forever.
Ownership	Just as human persons couldn't own other persons, corporations couldn't own the stock of other corporations (mergers and acquisitions were banned).	Corporations claim the human right to economic activity free of regulatory restraint, and the still-banned-for-humans right to own others of their own kind.

village" and corporate globalization. Of course, the influence of various groups and entities is nothing new. But today, the increasing size and wealth of corporations point to more concentration of wealth and of political and economic power and influence than before. Indeed, today as mentioned above, of the 100 largest economies in the world, 51 are corporations; only 49 are countries (based on a comparison of corporate sales and country GDPs).

Adam Smith, often regarded as the father of modern capitalism, wrote the influential famous book, The Wealth of Nations in 1776. This book exposed the mercantile and monopoly capitalism of the preceeding centuries as unjust and unfair, and proposed a free market system. He himself was very critical of the influences of concentrated ownership (which is also a way to reduce competition) and large corporations as interfering with free market capitalism (although many who do exert influence don't mind doing so in his name, and calling it free market!) Smith is worth quoting at length:

> Our merchants and master-manufacturers complain much of the bad effects of high wages in raising the price, and thereby lessening the sale of their good both at home and abroad. They say nothing concerning the bad effects of high profits. They are silent with regard to the pernicious effects of their own gains. They complain only of those of other people.
>
> [...]
>
> Merchants and master manufacturers are ... the two classes of people who commonly employ the largest capitals, and who by their wealth draw to themselves the greatest share of the public consideration. As during their whole lives they are engaged in plans and projects, they have frequently more acuteness of understanding than the greater part of country gentlemen. As their thoughts, however, are commonly exercised rather about the interest of their own particular branch of business, than about that of the society, their judgment, even when given with the greatest candour (which it has not been upon every occasion) is much more to be depended upon with regard to the former of those two objects than with regard to the latter. Their superiority over the country gentleman is not so much

in their knowledge of the public interest, as in their having a better knowledge of their own interest than he has of his. It is by this superior knowledge of their own interest that they have frequently imposed upon his generosity, and persuaded him to give up both his own interest and that of the public, from a very simple but honest conviction that their interest, and not his, was the interest of the public. The interest of the dealers, however, in any particular branch of trade or manufactures, is always in some respects different from, and even opposite to, that of the public. **To widen the market and to narrow the competition, is always the interest of the dealers.** To widen the market may frequently be agreeable enough to the interest of the public; but to narrow the competition must always be against it, and can serve only to enable the dealers, by raising their profits above what they naturally would be, to levy, for their own benefit, an absurd tax upon the rest of their fellow-citizens. **The proposal of any new law or regulation of commerce which comes from this order ought always to be listened to with great precaution, and ought never to be adopted till after having been long and carefully examined, not only with the most scrupulous, but with the most suspicious attention. It comes from an order of men whose interest is never exactly the same with that of the public, who have generally an interest to deceive and even to oppress the public, and who accordingly have, upon many occasions, both deceived and oppressed it.** (Emphasis Added)
—Adam Smith, The Wealth of Nations, Book I,
(Everyman's Library, Sixth Printing, 1991),
pp. 87-88, 231-232

As Adam Smith warns, only after great precaution, careful, scrupulous and suspicious attention should commerce-related policies from corporate interests be accepted. However, as described in detail on this web site's media section, corporations also have concentrated ownership of the mainstream media, which makes it even more difficult these days for the general public to apply great precaution, careful, scrupulous and suspicious attention.

VIEWPOINT 2

Small and Medium-Sized Businesses Need Less Regulation Than Large Ones

EurActive

In the following viewpoint, authors from EurActive examine a 2012 report on the relationship between a nation's economic performance and the number of large corporations that nation has. The study indicates that big corporations are more likely to do research and development. Regulations, the author says, that might be necessary for larger companies can stifle the growth of smaller ones. This, in turn, has a negative effect on the nation's economy as a whole.

As you read, consider the following questions:

1. According to this viewpoint what are the main reasons for slow company growth?
2. How does this author explain the interdependence of trade and innovation?
3. What sort of paradox does David Caro explain, as quoted in this piece?

Bigger corporations are more productive, they pay higher wages, enjoy higher profits, and are more successful in international

"Bigger Is Better: Large Companies Good for The Economy, Study Finds," EurActiv, August 29, 2012. Reprinted by permission.

markets, said the report by European Firms in a Global Economy (EFIGE), an EU-funded project.

Therefore, a country's economic performance can be linked to its number of big corporations, says the survey, which was carried out under the supervision of Brussels-based think tank Bruegel.

This is one of the conclusions in EFIGE's new report, Breaking down the barriers to firm growth in Europe. The report systematically explores the interaction between firm and country characteristics through a survey of about 15,000 manufacturers in Austria, France, Germany, Hungary, Italy, Spain and the United Kingdom.

Differences in the firm size profile of different European countries are dramatic, according to EFIGE. Companies in Spain and Italy are, for example, on average 40% smaller than those in Germany.

According to the authors of the report, it is important to understand the roots of the differences as they are "key to improving the economic performance of Europe's lagging economies."

The low-average firm size translates into a chronic lack of large firms. In Spain and Italy a mere 5% of manufacturing firms have more than 250 employees, compared to a much higher 11% in Germany. The average firm size in Spain and Italy is, respectively, 49.3 and 42.7 employees, compared to 76.4 on average in Germany.

Analysts Say Large Companies Are More Innovative

In all the countries in the survey, the exporting firms are also found to be larger and do more research and development (R&D).

"This suggests that barriers to R&D and trade are the main culprits that slow down firm growth. Countries that face higher trade costs provide fewer opportunities for businesses to become large. And a relative absence of R&D spending puts a break on firm growth, leading to a size distribution skewed towards smaller firms," the report said.

Trade and innovation are not independent, but interact in significant ways. For example, a reduction in trade costs tends to stimulate innovation as it allows firms to become larger. This makes it easier for the firm to bear the fixed costs of R&D.

To identify the barriers to firm growth, the authors behind the report say a model is needed to analyse different factors such as trade costs, innovation costs and tax distortions.

For example, if trade was to be ignored, then the model would predict that both Spain and Italy have high innovation costs. But once trade is introduced, the model finds that the large proportion of small firms in Italy is mainly due to high innovation costs, whereas in Spain it is due to a combination of high trade and high innovation costs.

If Italy wants to reduce the barriers to business growth, the country should mainly focus on promoting innovation. In Spain the emphasis should also be on cutting trade costs and improving access to international markets.

Positions

President of European Small Business Alliance (ESBA), a non-party political group, David Caro commented on the report:

"There is a paradox to be found here. We all agree that small and medium seized enterprises (SMEs) are the 'backbone of the European economy' and we look to our small companies to get us out of the crisis, yet large businesses still contribute disproportionately more to our economy. Unfortunately, this reaffirms the message that we have been voicing for years: cut down on the regulatory and administrative burden for SMEs, improve access to and cost of finance and allow small businesses to prosper, innovate and grow," Caro said.

"The one-size-fits-all approach does not work; small businesses cannot deal with the same rules and regulations as their large counterparts, which is why we need to fully implement the Think Small First principle once and for all. Less than one percent of EU businesses are large companies. The EU institutions have a responsibility to maximise the growth potential of the remaining 99% of European businesses, in order to become truly competitive," he added.

Background

The EU has adopted a 10-year growth plan, called "Europe 2020."

The strategy, agreed in June 2010 by the EU's heads of state, defined five "headline targets" that would need to be adapted at national level to reflect local differences:

- Raising the employment rate of the population aged 20-64 from the current 69% to 75%.

- Raising the investment in R&D to 3% of the EU's GDP.

- Meeting the EU's climate change and energy objective for 2020 to cut greenhouse gas emission by 20% and source 20% of its energy needs from renewable sources.

- Reducing the share of early school leavers from the current 15% to under 10% and making sure that at least 40% of youngsters have a degree or diploma.

- Reducing the number of Europeans living below the poverty line by 25%, lifting 20 million out of poverty from the current 80 million.

Viewpoint 3

In Tanzania Investment by China Brings Hope and Questions

Nick Van Mead

In recent years, China has been increasing trade with and investing more in African countries. In the following viewpoint, Nick Van Mead reports on a proposed project in Tanzania. (By the time you read this, the project will, after overcoming funding setbacks mentioned here, likely be well underway.) The author explores the potential consequences of China's investment in Africa and asks if the locals are right to be optimistic. China has promised that the project will bring much-needed improvements, such as schools, health centers, and better living conditions, yet the history of wealthy nations moving into poorer ones has not always gone well. Nick Van Mead is a writer and deputy editor of Guardian Cities.

As you read, consider the following questions:

1. What will fisherman like Chamume lose when the Chinese port comes in? What will they gain?
2. What is the Belt and Road Initiative, and what are the advantages for China?
3. What, according to this viewpoint, are some of the potential downsides of this type of project for Africans? What does the author mean by "new colonialism"?

"China in Africa: Win-Win Development, or a New Colonialism?" by Nick Van Mead, Guardian News and Media Limited, July 31, 2018. Reprinted by permission.

As their hand-built wooden dhow approaches the shore, Ibrahim Chamume and his fellow fishermen take in the sail and prepare to sell their catch to the small huddle of villagers waiting on the white sand. He has been making a living like this on the Indian Ocean since he was 14. His father was a fisherman, too.

Now in his 30s, Ibrahim says earning enough from traditional fishing is tough, but has its compensations. There is the view across the tranquil lagoon to the mangrove swamps; the unspoiled beaches and bays; the lush vegetation and smallholdings growing maize, cassava, cashews and mango. Such scenes must have played out in the tiny Tanzanian village of Mlingotini for centuries.

In a decade, however, the mud-and-thatch homes of Mlingotini, and a further four villages along this coastline 30 miles north of Dar Es Salaam, will be gone—razed to make space for a $10bn Chinese-built mega-port and a special economic zone backed by an Omani sovereign wealth fund.

The area south of Bagamoyo—once notorious as a key staging point in the slave trade and unsuccessfully proposed 12 years ago as a world heritage site—is seen by China as a new Shenzhen. Before Deng Xiaoping designated Shenzhen as China's first special economic zone in 1979, it, too, was just a small fishing town. Now it is a hi-tech hub and one of the world's biggest cities.

Bagamoyo, if the project goes ahead as planned, will be transformed into the largest port in Africa. That is looking ever more likely: after years of delay, the Tanzanian government says it is in the final stages of talks with state-run China Merchants Holdings International.

The lagoon will be dredged, to allow access to the vast cargo ships that will queue many miles out to sea. As for the special economic zone, the original masterplan shows factories in a fenced-off industrial area, and apartment blocks to accommodate the estimated future population of 75,000. There is even talk of an international airport. Many of the villagers have already accepted compensation for the loss of their homes.

The comparison with Shenzhen may not be so far-fetched, says the China-Africa specialist Lauren Johnston of New South Economics. "Would visitors to Shenzhen in 1980 have believed what would be unlocked by that sleepy port?" she says. "Bagamoyo could become an industrial gateway not only for youth-filled Tanzania but half a dozen landlocked African countries. There are parallels."

The proposed radical transformation of the Bagamoyo coastline is an unofficial extension to east Africa as part of Chinese president Xi Jinping's Belt and Road Initiative—and is just the latest in a long line of China-in-Africa projects. Ahead of next month's China-Africa summit, foreign minister Wang Yi is inviting African leaders to "get on board the fast train of development."

It is now nine years since China overtook the US as Africa's largest trading partner. Although Kenya and Ethiopia were the only two African nations among the 30 countries signing economic and trade agreements at the Belt and Road Forum (Barf) in Beijing in May last year, China has been busy on the continent.

The flagship Belt and Road project is Kenya's 290-mile railway from the capital, Nairobi, to the port city of Mombasa, which opened to the public last year. There are plans to extend that network into South Sudan, Uganda, Rwanda and Burundi; it was already the country's largest infrastructure project since independence.

Meanwhile, landlocked Ethiopia got a 470-mile electric railway from its capital, Addis Ababa, to the port in the neighbouring dictatorship of Djibouti. The £2.5bn project—financed by a Chinese bank and built by Chinese companies—opened in January. Addis's new light rail system, too, was funded and built by China, and operated by Shenzhen Metro Group. And Djibouti, in exchange for major investments, preferential loans, a pipeline and two airports, got China's first overseas military base.

While east Africa has been the main focus of Belt and Road on the continent, Chinese infrastructure projects stretch all the way to Angola and Nigeria, with ports planned along the coast from Dakar to Libreville and Lagos. Beijing has also signalled its support for the African Union's proposal of a pan-African high-speed rail network.

Where does China in Africa end, and Belt and Road begin? Professor Steve Tsang, director of the Soas China Institute, says the definition is vague—but getting too caught up in that misses the point. "If you'd like a project to be Belt and Road, it can be Belt and Road," he says. "You can fit anything into it. It's a way of getting support for your project."

Mao's Mega-Project Reborn?

The new port of Bagamoyo could see the revival of what Tsang calls "the very first China in Africa mega-project": the Tazara railway line, stretching from the copper mines of Zambia to Dar Es Salaam.

Tazara dates back to the 1960s, when Chairman Mao Zedong won friends on the continent by supporting anti-colonial movements such as that of Julius Nyerere in Tanzania. The 1,100-mile railway opened to much fanfare in 1976—it was the first infrastructure project conceived on a pan-African scale.

Four decades later, the once-grand station in Dar Es Salaam stands empty most days, its missing ceiling panels exposing rotting beams and allowing water to pool on the floor. Two rusty trains a week rattle up and down the line. In the cavernous main hall, a few people wait under broken TV screens for an express service which is running nine hours late.

But the old line could "shine again," promised former Chinese ambassador Lu Youqing. There is a proposed extension to Bagamoyo, and a plan to link a revamped Tazara to landlocked Malawi, Rwanda, and Burundi. The railway's chief executive has talked excitedly of 125mph trains.

The key difference is that Tazara was mostly paid for by Chinese aid money—a significant investment given how impoverished China was at the time. Whether branded Belt and Road or not, virtually every new project is now funded by Chinese commercial loans.

There have been concerns about these loans. Research by the Centre for Global Development found Djibouti was among eight Belt and Road countries significantly or highly vulnerable to debt distress from the loans—with IMF figures showing its public external debt swelling from 50% to 85% of GDP in two years. Before his visit to Africa in March, former US secretary of state Rex Tillerson accused China of predatory loan practices; when she was secretary of state, Hillary Clinton warned of China's "new colonialism." Four months into the job, Tillerson's successor Mike Pompeo is yet to visit.

Though China loaned a whopping $95.5bn on the continent between 2000 and 2015, researchers at the China Africa Research Initiative found most of this was spent addressing Africa's infrastructure gap. Some 40% of the Chinese loans paid for power projects, and another 30% went on modernising transport infrastructure. The loans were at comparatively low interest rates and with long repayment periods.

"The risk for African borrowers relates to the project's profitability," says Cari director Deborah Bräutigam. "Will they be able to generate enough economic activity through these projects to repay these loans? Or are the projects seen more as ribbon-cutting opportunities? The Chinese believe that ports and special economic zones are a 'win-win' development tool. It's what they did at home at an earlier stage of their development."

Many African people certainly see grounds for optimism. Almost two-thirds of Tanzanians view China favourably, compared with less than half of Europeans and Americans, according to the Pew Research Center.

As Bagamoyo readies for a seismic transformation from sleepy town to mega-port, the residents seem to feel unanimously positive. From the taxi drivers in the old town in their starched white kanzu cotton robes to the fashionable young restaurant manager, all were confident they would profit from more businesses, more offices, more jobs, more money. The original masterplan includes talk of schools and health centres, playgrounds and fibre-optic broadband.

Even the fishermen—whose quiet lives look set to be turned upside down—seem optimistic. Despite concerns that the compensation already paid in connection with the special economic zone was not enough to relocate, most thought the new wealth would somehow trickle down. "It will bring many benefits," says Ibrahim Chamume as we shelter under a thatched roof from a tropical downpour. His first child died young but he and his wife hope to have more. "Even if I do not prosper, they will."

VIEWPOINT 4

In Africa, the Country's Colonial History Affects Its Development

Ewout Frankema

In the following viewpoint Ewout Frankema takes a deeper look at Africa's colonial history. After discussing the history of European colonization in Africa, the author points out that China's recent investment in the region might be a replay of European colonialism of Africa in previous eras. However, he ends on a positive note, suggesting steps African nations themselves might take to avoid the mistakes of the past. Ewout Frankema is professor and chair of rural and environmental history at Wageningen University and Research in The Netherlands.

As you read, consider the following questions:

1. Does the author of this viewpoint believe that the history discussed here foreshadows what may come from China's increased intervention in Africa?
2. What does the author mean by "commodity dependency," and what are the potential consequences for African nations?
3. What, according to this viewpoint, can African leaders do to avoid the mistakes of the past?

The supply of African slaves to American plantations reached an all-time high in the late 18th century (Klein 1999). After anti-

"How Africa's Colonial History Affects Its Development," by Ewout Frankema, World Economic Forum, July 15, 2015. Reprinted by permission.

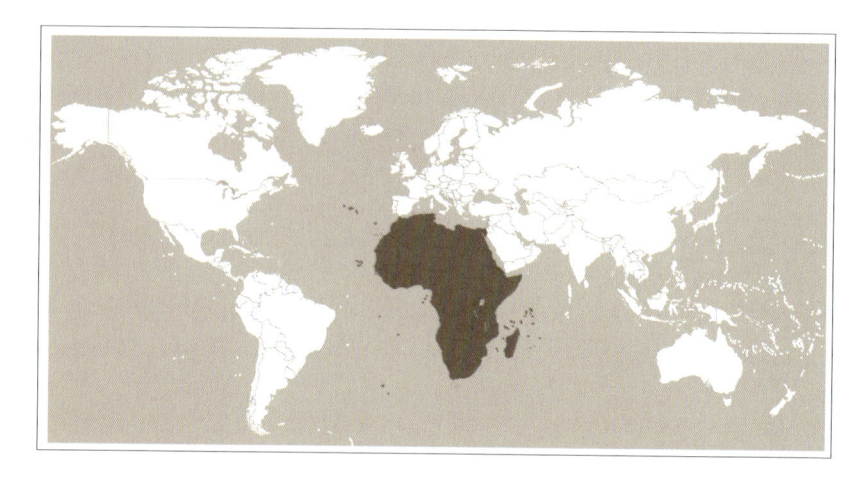

slave trade legislation finally shut down the Atlantic slave exports, commodity exports filled the gap. This so-called "commercial transition" was completed in West Africa before it hit East Africa (Austen 1987, Law 2002). It was a game-changer, since it put a halt to the continuous drain of scarce labour and paved the way for the expansion of land-intensive forms of tropical agriculture, engaging smallholders, communal farms, and estates.

The establishment of colonial rule over the African interior (c. 1880-1900) reinforced Africa's commodity export growth. Colonial control facilitated the construction of railways, induced large inflows of European investment, and forced profound changes in the operation of labour and land markets (Frankema and van Waijenburg 2012). That is, colonial regimes abolished slavery, but they replaced it with other forced labour schemes. The scramble pushed African exports to new heights, but without the preceding era of commercialisation the African scramble probably would never have taken place.

The Industrial Revolution

Africa's commercial transition was inextricably connected to the rising demand for industrial inputs from the industrialising core in the North Atlantic. Revolutions in transportation (railways, steamships), a move towards liberal trade policies in Europe, and increasing rates of GDP growth enhanced demand for (new) manufactures, raw materials and tropical cash crops. African producers responded to this demand by increasing exports of vegetable oils (palm oil, groundnuts), gum, ivory, gold, hides and skins. Palm oil, a key export, was highly valued as a lubricant for machinery and an ingredient in food and soap. During and after the scramble, the range of commodity exports broadened to include raw materials like rubber, cotton, and copper, as well as cash crops such as cocoa, coffee, tea and tobacco. The lion's share of these commodities went directly to manufacturing firms and consumers in Europe. Meanwhile, technological innovations also reduced the costs of colonial occupation. These included the Maxim gun, the steamship, the railway and quinine, the latter lowering the health risks to Europeans in the disease-ridden interior of the "dark continent."

The African Trade Boom

To obtain a deeper understanding of the connection between Africa's commercial transition and subsequent colonial intervention, we constructed annual time-series of export volumes, export values, commodity export prices, import prices, and the net barter terms (the ratio of average export to average import prices). The data cover the period from the heyday of the Atlantic slave trade in the 1790s to the eve of World War II,[1] and make it possible to analyse the commercial transition with much greater precision than was possible previously and to compare the development of African trade with other commodity exporting regions (Williamson 2011).

There was a prolonged rise in the net barter terms of trade for sub-Saharan Africa from the 1790s to the 1880s, a commodity price boom that was especially pronounced in the four decades between 1845 and 1885. This secular price boom peaked exactly at the date of the Berlin conference (1884-5), when diplomats negotiated how to carve up Africa among the European imperialists. The terms of trade tripled in just four decades. While the terms of trade for commodity exporters were rising everywhere in what was once called the Third World, nowhere was the boom greater than for Africa. Furthermore, the scramble started right at the moment when African exports reached their highest exchange value.

The share of West African exports in French imperial trade was much larger than it was in British imperial trade. Around the mid-19th century, about two thirds of French imperial trade was with Africa, the largest part of it with North Africa (e.g. Algeria), but a substantial share was also with West Africa. British imperial trade was dominated by India, and this distinction is consistent with the chronology of the scramble. The French set a chain reaction in motion by moving into the West African interior to survey the possibilities of a railway connection between the major trading hubs of the middle Niger delta (Gao, Timbuktu) and their trading enclaves along the Senegalese coast. The British responded by securing the lower Niger delta. After less than two decades, virtually the entire continent was divided among a handful of European powers.

Africa's Commodity Boom in Global Perspective

The long-term secular trend of sub-Saharan Africa's terms of trade coincided with the patterns observed in other parts of the commodity-exporting periphery. However, the price boom of 1845-1885 was exceptionally sharp compared with Latin America, Southeast Asia, India and China. From start to peak, the purchasing power of African exports rose by 3% per annum. Although Africa's share of world exports remained modest, the trend fuelled an optimistic assessment of the future profitability of colonisation, French assessments in particular. Merchants, industrial capitalists, explorers (like David Livingstone) and even Christian missionaries added to the babble about new markets, new investment prospects, new converts, and the moral obligation to abolish African slavery and replace it with a commercial model.

Did Colonisation Lock Africa into a Perverse Path of Specialisation?

Ironically, the secular terms of trade boom turned into an equally prolonged bust right at the time that the scramble gained steam. This price bust continued, with only some temporary reversals, up to the eve of World War II. In fact, in 1940 Africa's terms of trade were back at their 1800 levels. Table 1 below shows that export volumes continued to expand after 1885 at a faster pace than before, thus offsetting the price declines. In other words, African farmers, European planters and mining firms specialised more and more in commodities as they became worth less and less.

Table 1. Decomposition of export growth in British and French West Africa, 1850-1929

	Annual growth of purchasing power of exports	Price contribution to annual growth	Volume contribution to annual growth
British West Africa			
1850-1885	3.8	46%	54%
1885-1929	5.5	-24%	124%
French West Africa			
1850-1885	5.0	72%	28%
1885-1929	2.0	-123%	223%

Does this mean that European colonisation locked Africa into a path of perverse specialisation? There are two plausible answers to this question: "yes" and "no". The "yes" view is that expanding imports of European manufactures, coercive cultivation and mining schemes, and free-trade policies effectively pre-empted a diversification of African economies into manufacturing and eroded indigenous handicrafts. Only white-dominated settler economies that were able to operate with some degree of autonomy, such as South Africa and Southern Rhodesia, managed to develop a substantial industrial sector, albeit relying on a combination of protective barriers and African labour coercion. The alternative answer is "no". Colonial trade simply followed a path that had already been blazed in the early 19th century. Manufacturing was inconsistent with African endowments and thus its comparative advantage. With abundant land and mineral resources, and scarce labour and human capital, commodity specialisation was the most efficient way to exploit world trade, and to move up the technology and skill ladder (Austin et al. 2016). The debate between these two competing views has not yet been resolved.

Is History Repeating?

Today, China uses diplomacy in Africa instead of brute force, and it does not seem to aspire to formal political control in the region. Yet, African economies are again responding to the rising demand for commodities by a rapidly industrialising power. Chinese investments in land, infrastructure and mines are flowing in. Mineral exports, and especially oil, are again taking a growing share of African exports. History shows that such export booms are unsustainable, but what are the chances that Africa will avoid a renewed cycle of commodity dependency? As we ponder the answer, a major difference with history should be noted. With a projected population of over 3 billion, Africa will be one of the most populous regions of the world in 2050. If African policymakers find ways to invest commodity windfalls in the health and education of the next generations and to increase trade with neighbour countries, export growth may do more to stimulate African economic development than it did a century ago.

References

Austen, R A (1987), African Economic History: Internal Development and External Dependency, London: James Curry/Heinemann.

Austin G, E Frankema and M Jerven (2016), "Patterns of Manufacturing Growth in Sub-Saharan Africa: From Colonization to the Present," forthcoming in K O'Rourke and J G

Williamson (eds), The Spread of Modern Manufacturing to the Periphery, 1870 to the Present, Oxford: Oxford University Press.

Frankema E, J G Williamson and P Woltjer (2015), "An economic rationale for the African scramble: the commercial transition and the commodity price boom of 1845-1885." NBER Working Paper 21213.

Frankema, E H P and M Van Waijenburg (2012), "Structural Impediments to African Growth? New Evidence from Real Wages in British Africa, 1880-1965", Journal of Economic History 72(4), pp. 895-926.

Klein, H S (1999), The Atlantic slave trade, Cambridge, UK: Cambridge University Press.

Law, R (2002), From slave trade to legitimate commerce: the commercial transition in nineteenth-century West Africa, Cambridge, UK: Cambridge University Press.

Williamson, J G (2011), Trade and poverty when the Third World fell behind, Cambridge MA: MIT Press.

Footnote

1. These data will be made available as part of Wageningen African Commodity Trade Database, 1500-present, to be released in the autumn of 2015 at the website of the African Economic History Network, www.aehnetwork.org

VIEWPOINT 5

In Brazil an Election Shows That True Power Lies with Corporations, Not Nations

Gary Younge

In the following viewpoint Gary Younge describes the events surrounding the 2002 election of Luiz Inácio Lula da Silva. Lula was elected on the promise of fighting poverty and redistributing wealth and the response of the global economic order to his election. The author goes on to explain how corporations are more powerful in international affairs than are nation states. Gary Younge is editor at large for the Guardian *and columnist for the* Nation.

As you read, consider the following questions:

1. What did Luiz Inácio Lula da Silva's aide mean when he said "We are in government but not in power"?
2. What is the problem, according to Younge, with describing far right parties as "racist"?
3. How does this essay explain the emergence of intolerance in countries where democracy has been subverted by corporate interests?

The night in 2002 when Luiz Inácio Lula da Silva won his landslide victory in Brazil's presidential elections, he warned supporters: "So far, it has been easy. The hard part begins now."

"Who's in Control—Nation States or Global Corporations?" by Gary Younge, Guardian News and Media Limited, June 2, 2014. Reprinted by permission.

He wasn't wrong. As head of the leftwing Workers' party he was elected on a platform of fighting poverty and redistributing wealth. A year earlier, the party had produced a document, Another Brazil is Possible, laying out its electoral programme. In a section entitled "The Necessary Rupture," it argued: "Regarding the foreign debt, now predominantly private, it will be necessary to denounce the agreement with the IMF, in order to free the economic policy from the restrictions imposed on growth and on the defence of Brazilian commercial interests."

But on the way to Lula's inauguration the invisible hand of the market tore up his electoral promises and boxed the country around the ears for its reckless democratic choice. In the three months between his winning and being sworn in, the currency plummeted by 30%, $6bn in hot money left the country, and some agencies gave Brazil the highest debt-risk ratings in the world. "We are in government but not in power," said Lula's close aide, Dominican friar Frei Betto. "Power today is global power, the power of the big companies, the power of financial capital."

The limited ability of national governments to pursue any agenda that has not first been endorsed by international capital and its proxies is no longer simply the cross they have to bear; it is the cross to which we have all been nailed. The nation state is the primary democratic entity that remains. But given the scale of neoliberal globalisation it is clearly no longer up to that task.

"By many measures, corporations are more central players in global affairs than nations," writes Benjamin Barber in Jihad vs McWorld. "We call them multinational but they are more accurately understood as postnational, transnational or even anti-national. For they abjure the very idea of nations or any other parochialism that limits them in time or space."

This contradiction is not new. Indeed, it is precisely because it has continued, challenged but virtually unchecked, for more than a generation, that political cynicism has intensified.

"The crisis consists precisely in the fact that the old is dying and the new cannot be born," argued the Italian Marxist Antonio Gramsci. "In this interregnum a great variety of morbid symptoms appear."

The recent success of the far right in the European parliamentary elections revealed just how morbid those symptoms have become. Nationalist and openly xenophobic parties topped the polls in three countries—Denmark, France and the UK—and won more than 10% in another five. These victories, election to a parliament with little real power, on a very low turnout, can be overstated. Ukip won just 9% of the eligible electorate, the Front National 10.6% and the Danish People's party 15%. But the trend should not be underplayed. Over the past 30 years, fascism—and its 57 varieties of fellow travellers in denial—has shifted as a political current from marginal to mainstream to central in Europe's political culture.

The problem with describing these parties as racist is not that the description is inaccurate but that, by itself, it is inadequate. For their appeal lies in a far broader set of anxieties about the degree to which our politics and economics are shaped by forces accountable to none and controlled by a few: a drift towards cosmopolitanism in which citizens, once relatively secure in their national identity and financial wellbeing, are excluded from the polity.

The responses to these anxieties have been racially problematic. But the anxieties themselves are well-founded. From the Seattle protests over a decade ago, to the Occupy movement more recently, the left has been grappling with the same crisis. The recent elections produced less impressive but nonetheless significant successes for the hard left. In six countries, socialist-oriented groups critical of neoliberal globalisation got double figures, including Syriza, which topped the poll in Greece. They are also Eurosceptic. However, their base is driven not by a dislike of foreigners but by a desire for more democracy in the EU and more national autonomy.

"It seems clear that … nationalism is not only not a spent force," argued the late Stuart Hall in an essay, Our Mongrel Selves. "It isn't necessarily either a reactionary or a progressive force, politically." It suits the far right to shroud its racial animus within these blurred distinctions in order to appear more moderate. "Our people demand one type of politics: they want politics by the French, for the French, with the French," said Front National leader Marine Le Pen in her victory speech. "They don't want to be led any more from outside. What is happening in France heralds what will happen in all European countries, the return of the nation."

That is unlikely. Quite how these parties turn the clock back and what year they would set it to is not clear. Neither the right nor the left has a solution for this crisis. But while the left holds out hope of building a more inclusive society in the future, the right has built its populist credentials on retreating to an exclusionary past.

In the absence of any serious strategy to protect democracy the right resorts, instead, to a defence of "culture"—reinvented as "tradition", elevated to "heritage" and imagined as immutable. Having evoked the myth of purity it then targets the human pollutants—low-skilled immigrants, Gypsies, Muslims, take your pick. People who wouldn't know a credit default swap if it ran up and kicked them out of their house, but who are as accessible and identifiable as neoliberal globalisation—that force without a face—is elusive.

"Minorities are the flashpoint for a series of uncertainties that mediate between everyday life and its fast-shifting global backdrop," writes Arjun Appadurai in Fear of Small Numbers. "This uncertainty, exacerbated by an inability of states to secure economic sovereignty in the era of globalisation, can translate into a lack of tolerance of any sort of collective stranger." The targets of this intolerance shift according to the context: Roma in Hungary, Romanians in Britain, Latinos in the US and Muslims almost everywhere in the west. But the rhetoric and the true nature of the crisis remain constant. Parochial identities describe the protagonists, but it is global economics that shapes the narrative.

VIEWPOINT 6

In China and the United States a Trade War Poses Risks

Charles Hankla

The two previous viewpoints have been concerned with the growing power of international corporations and their economic dominance. In the following viewpoint, Charles Hankla analyzes the trade war with China begun by US president Donald Trump. The author illustrates how international economics influences political situations in ways that are not always obvious and can lead to shifting alliances and geopolitical conflicts that go far beyond trade. Charles Hankla is associate professor of political science at Georgia State University,

As you read, consider the following questions:

1. Though the US imports far more goods from China than China does from the United States, Hankla argues that China still has leverage over the United States. What examples does he give?
2. What advantage, according to this viewpoint, would there have been for China in avoiding confrontation until after the 2020 elections?
3. In this viewpoint the trade war is likely to have effects far beyond tit-for-tat tariffs. How are geopolitical relations affected by trade issues?

"The Next Cold War? US-China Trade War Risks Something Worse," by Charles Hankla, The Conversation, September 24, 2018. https://theconversation.com/the-next-cold-war-us-china-trade-war-risks-something-worse-103733. Licensed under CC BY 4.0 International.

The Dominance of Global Corporations

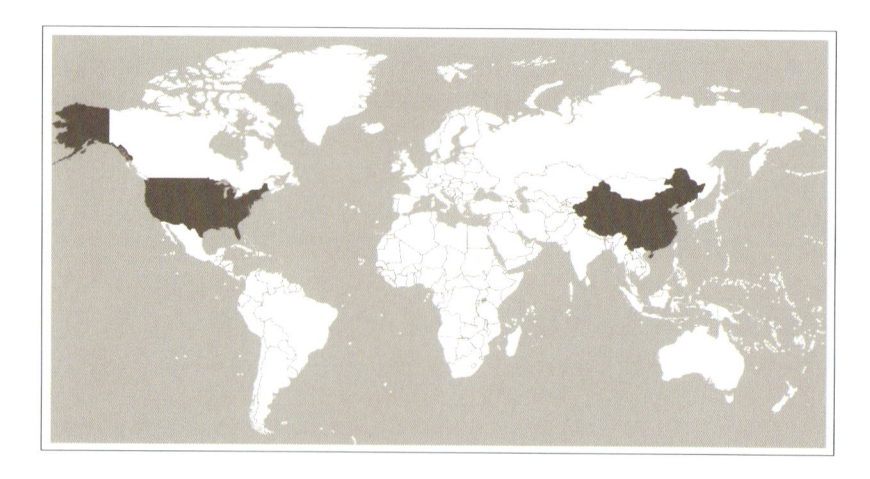

President Donald Trump is making good on his pledge to escalate the trade war with China by imposing tariffs on US$200 billion of Chinese goods. The Chinese government, for its part, is already retaliating with new taxes on $60 billion of American imports.

If you're curious why China's sanctions don't match Trump's, there's an easy explanation. As a number of commentators have correctly pointed out, Beijing is running out of American products to target. Americans bought $375 billion more stuff from China than the Chinese bought from the U.S. last year, which means Trump has a lot more to punish.

While this may mean that China's leverage on trade is limited, it doesn't mean that Trump can easily win this confrontation.

That's because China has many other ways to retaliate, such as dumping its considerable holdings of U.S. debt or making it harder for Trump to get a nuclear deal with North Korea. In these and other areas, Beijing has enormous leverage. This has led some to suggest that the trade war may soon turn into a "new cold war."

Could the U.S. and China really be on the verge of the kind of geopolitical stalemate that dominated the second half of the 20th century?

Much will depend on how China responds to the latest tariffs. I believe that this response could take four forms.

Cooler Heads

First, China could choose to de-escalate the confrontation. This could be done quickly by negotiating some resolution with the Trump administration—though the president's terms for ending the trade war remain unclear.

Alternatively, China could let the conflict simmer by keeping the fight in the trade arena, allowing it to continue to retaliate while appearing "reasonable." This approach would avoid any major embarrassment for China while kicking the dispute down the road in the hope that the November elections, or the 2020 presidential elections, will soften American policy. In fact, China has already said that it won't negotiate until after the midterms.

A conciliatory strategy might be attractive to moderates in Beijing who are keenly aware that China needs the U.S. as much as the U.S. needs China. It would also reassure China's other trading partners that it is serious about honoring its commitments.

Economic Pain

Another option for China is to escalate the confrontation by using its substantial economic leverage outside of trade.

The most obvious way that China could retaliate would be by reducing its purchases of American Treasuries or by selling some of the $1.18 trillion in its possession. Overall, China owns almost a fifth of the U.S. national debt currently held by foreign countries.

Though it would probably be less apocalyptic than is sometimes assumed, a Chinese policy of reducing its holdings would substantially drive up the cost of many of the goods that Americans buy every day.

The problem with this approach for China is that it would also strengthen the yuan and make Chinese goods more expensive for foreigners. Such a form of financial retaliation may not be a credible option for Beijing.

A more feasible strategy would be to target U.S. companies operating in China with more regulations and interference. While such targeting would be contrary to international law, it would be fairly easy for Beijing to deny responsibility.

Indeed, there is reason to believe that China has used this approach before with South Korean corporations—and there are indications that it has already begun delaying license applications from American companies.

Geopolitical Games

The U.S. relationship with China is multifaceted, a fact that could allow China to retaliate outside the economic arena altogether.

One way would be to use its influence with North Korea to undermine U.S. efforts to disarm Kim Jong Un, perhaps by not enforcing U.S. sanctions.

Or China could confront the U.S. in the South China Sea, probably the most dangerous strategic flashpoint in East Asia. As Beijing rushes to claim more islands and seaways south of its coast, a falling out with the United States over trade could encourage it to become even more belligerent.

Other options would be to ramp up its attempts to isolate Taiwan, deepen ties with Russia as a counterbalance to the U.S. or accelerate its military buildup.

Hegemony on Steroids

Finally, China could take America's aggressive approach on trade as a reason to speed up its efforts to establish regional hegemony and greater economic independence.

The China 2025 program, a set of industrial policies aimed at moving the country closer to the technological frontier, could get a boost from the confrontation. China's famous "Belt and Road Initiative," an enormous economic corridor funded by Beijing, could be expanded, as could the country's efforts to grow its influence in Africa. China could also pump more cash into its alternative to the World Bank, the Asian Infrastructure Development Bank.

Of course, China has sought to grow its influence, using all of the mechanisms discussed above, for some time. A more aggressive United States, however, could add to China's sense of urgency.

What Will China Do?

The most likely Chinese response, in my judgment as a political economist, is some mixture of all four options.

Keeping the confrontation limited to trade—at least on the surface—is the safest bet for China's leaders. And so I expect that Beijing will reserve its overt retaliation for tariffs. At the same time, I anticipate that China will engage in other noticeable but more informal and deniable actions against U.S economic and security interests—from causing headaches for American companies to building up its military.

In short, the Chinese government will seek to expand its powers so that it is able to deter future threats like these from the United States.

A Different Kind of Cold War

In other words, President Trump is playing a risky game of whack-a-mole. In trying to tackle the trade deficit with a sledgehammer, he's creating a host of other serious challenges to U.S. interests that may persist for years to come.

The enormous and persistent U.S. trade deficit with China needs a solution, but tariffs aren't it. A wiser American approach would be to use the existing mechanisms of the international order to resolve its legitimate trade grievances with China.

And there are other ways to reduce the trade deficit and mitigate its ill effects, such as by encouraging higher savings rates, cutting the federal deficit (made worse by Trump's tax cuts) and promoting competitiveness through job retraining and investment.

But back to our original question, are we heading for a new cold war?

In short, no, at least not the kind fought between the U.S. and Soviet Union after World War II. The Cold War may have been frozen in Europe, but it led, directly or indirectly, to terrible conflicts in Korea, Vietnam and beyond. It also divided the world into two mutually antagonistic blocs constantly struggling for the upper hand.

Certainly, a growing conflict between the world's two largest powers could again encourage the formation of opposing spheres of influence. But the economic interdependence between the U.S. and China—as well as the existence of other major powers—would make such a "cold war" quite different, and probably milder, than the previous one.

Nevertheless, it is better for the U.S. to avoid a confrontational relationship with China altogether. It's natural to defend one's interests, but an escalating fight, leading who knows where, would benefit no one.

Periodical and Internet Sources Bibliography

The following articles have been selected to supplement the diverse views presented in this chapter.

Milan Babic, et al, "States versus Corporations: Rethinking the Power of Business in International Politics," *Italian Journal of International Affairs*, volume 52, 2017, issue 4. https://www.tandfonline.com/doi/full/10.1080/03932729.2017.1389151

Caleb Crain, "Is Capitalism a Threat to Democracy?" *New Yorker*, May 7, 2018. https://www.newyorker.com/magazine/2018/05/14/is-capitalism-a-threat-to-democracy

Lee Drutman, "How Corporate Lobbyists Conquered American Democracy," *Atlantic*, April 20, 2015. https://www.theatlantic.com/business/archive/2015/04/how-corporate-lobbyists-conquered-american-democracy/390822/

Greg Kaufmann, "The Plan to Save Our Economy," *Nation*, April 15, 2019. https://www.thenation.com/article/roosevelt-institute-stacey-abrams-economy-inequality-report/

Stacy Mitchell, "Elizabeth Warren Has a Theory about Corporate Power," *Atlantic*, May 16, 2019. https://amp.theatlantic.com/amp/article/589510/

Asher Schechter, "How Market Power Leads to Corporate Political Influence," Pro-Market, July 12, 2017. https://promarket.org/market-power-leads-corporate-political-influence/

Jon Basil Utley, "How America Benefits from World Trade, *American Conservative*, May 10, 2018. https://www.theamericanconservative.com/articles/how-america-benefits-from-world-trade/

Robert Verbruggen, "How Corporations Won Their Civil Rights," *American Conservative*, July 3, 2018. https://www.theamericanconservative.com/articles/how-corporations-won-their-civil-rights/

Chapter 2

Causes and Effects of Global Corporate Dominance

VIEWPOINT 1

Globalization Is Not Living Up to Its Promise

Gail Tverberg

In the following viewpoint, Gail Tverberg argues that the realities of globalization have had a negative effect on the world. The author discusses twelve problems caused by globalization, particularly focusing on the environmental problems created by a globalized economy. Gail Tverberg is a researcher who specializes in studying how energy limits and the economy are interconnected. She is the author of many academic papers and editor of the blog Our Finite World.

As you read, consider the following questions:

1. Why, according to this author, does globalization use up more resources and produce more pollution than local economies?
2. What does Tverberg say are the challenge for regulators in a globalized economy?
3. How, according to this author, does globalization shift tax burden from corporations to citizens?

Globalization seems to be looked on as an unmitigated "good" by economists. Unfortunately, economists seem to be guided by their badly flawed models; they miss real-world problems. In particular, they miss the point that the world is finite. We don't have

"Twelve Reasons Why Globalization Is a Huge Problem," by Gail Tverberg, OurFiniteWorld.com, February 22, 2013. Reprinted by permission.

infinite resources, or unlimited ability to handle excess pollution. So we are setting up a "solution" that is at best temporary.

Economists also tend to look at results too narrowly–from the point of view of a business that can expand, or a worker who has plenty of money, even though these users are not typical. In real life, businesses are facing increased competition, and the worker may be laid off because of greater competition.

The following is a list of reasons why globalization is not living up to what was promised, and is, in fact, a very major problem.

1. Globalization Uses Up Finite Resources More Quickly

As an example, China joined the world trade organization in December 2001. In 2002, its coal use began rising rapidly.

In fact, there is also a huge increase in world coal consumption. India's consumption is increasing as well, but from a smaller base.

2. Globalization Increases World Carbon Dioxide Emissions

If the world burns its coal more quickly, and does not cut back on other fossil fuel use, carbon dioxide emissions increase. Carbon dioxide emissions have increased, relative to what might have been expected, based on the trend line for the years prior to when the Kyoto protocol was adopted in 1997.

3. Globalization Makes it Virtually Impossible for Regulators in One Country to Foresee the Worldwide Implications of Their Actions

Actions which would seem to reduce emissions for an individual country may indirectly encourage world trade, ramp up manufacturing in coal-producing areas, and increase emissions over all. See my post Climate Change: Why Standard Fixes Don't Work.

4. Globalization Acts to Increase World Oil Prices

The world has undergone two sets of oil price spikes. The first one, in the 1973 to 1983 period, occurred after US oil supply began to decline in 1970.

After 1983, it was possible to bring oil prices back to the $30 to $40 barrel range (in 2012$), compared to the $20 barrel price (in 2012$) available prior to 1970. This was partly done partly by ramping up oil production in the North Sea, Alaska and Mexico (sources which were already known), and partly by reducing consumption. The reduction in consumption was accomplished by cutting back oil use for electricity, and by encouraging the use of more fuel-efficient cars.

Now, since 2005, we have high oil prices back, but we have a much worse problem. The reason the problem is worse now is partly because oil supply is not growing very much, due to limits we are reaching, and partly because demand is exploding due to globalization.

If we look at world oil supply, it is virtually flat. The United States and Canada together provide the slight increase in world oil supply that has occurred since 2005. Otherwise, supply has been flat since 2005. What looks like a huge increase in US oil production in 2012 looks much less impressive, when viewed in the context of world oil production.

Part of our problem now is that with globalization, world oil demand is rising very rapidly. Chinese buyers purchased more cars in 2012 than did European buyers. Rapidly rising world demand, together with oil supply which is barely rising, pushes world prices upward. This time, there also is no possibility of a dip in world oil demand of the type that occurred in the early 1980s. Even if the West drops its oil consumption greatly, the East has sufficient pent-up demand that it will make use of any oil that is made available to the market.

Adding to our problem is the fact that we have already extracted most of the inexpensive to extract oil because the "easy" (and cheap) to extract oil was extracted first. Because of this, oil prices cannot decrease very much, without world supply dropping off. Instead, because of diminishing returns, needed price keeps ratcheting upward. The new "tight" oil that is acting to increase US supply is an example of expensive to produce oil–it can't bring needed price relief.

5. Globalization Transfers Consumption of Limited Oil Supply from Developed Countries to Developing Countries

If world oil supply isn't growing by very much, and demand is growing rapidly in developing countries, oil to meet this rising demand must come from somewhere. The way this transfer takes place is through the mechanism of high oil prices. High oil prices are particularly a problem for major oil importing countries, such as the United States, many European countries, and Japan. Because oil is used in growing food and for commuting, a rise in oil price tends to lead to a cutback in discretionary spending, recession, and lower oil use in these countries. See my academic article, "Oil Supply Limits and the Continuing Financial Crisis," (https://oilprice.com/Finance/the-Economy/12-Negative-Aspects-of-Globalization.html).

Developing countries are better able to use higher-priced oil than developed countries. In some cases (particularly in oil-producing countries) subsidies play a role. In addition, the shift of manufacturing to less developed countries increases the number of workers who can afford a motorcycle or car. Job loss plays a role in the loss of oil consumption from developed countries–see my post, Why is US Oil Consumption Lower? Better Gasoline Mileage? (https://ourfiniteworld.com/2013/01/31/why-is-us-oil-consumption-lower-better-gasoline-mileage/) The real issue isn't better mileage; one major issue is loss of jobs.

6. Globalization Transfers Jobs from Developed Countries to Less Developed Countries

Globalization levels the playing field, in a way that makes it hard for developed countries to compete. A country with a lower cost structure (lower wages and benefits for workers, more inexpensive coal in its energy mix, and more lenient rules on pollution) is able to out-compete a typical OECD country. In the United States, the percentage of US citizen with jobs started dropping about the time China joined the World Trade Organization in 2001.

7. Globalization Transfers Investment Spending from Developed Countries to Less Developed Countries

If an investor has a chance to choose between a country with a competitive advantage and a country with a competitive disadvantage, which will the investor choose? A shift in investment shouldn't be too surprising.

In the US, domestic investment was fairly steady as a percentage of National Income until the mid-1980s. In recent years, it has dropped off and is now close to consumption of assets (similar to depreciation, but includes other removal from service). The assets in question include all types of capital assets, including government-owned assets (schools, roads), business owned assets (factories, stores), and individual homes. A similar pattern applies to business investment viewed separately.

Part of the shift in the balance between investment and consumption of assets is rising consumption of assets. This would include early retirement of factories, among other things.

Even very low interest rates in recent years have not brought US investment back to earlier levels.

How to Avoid the Harms Without Sacrificing the Benefits of Globalization

Proponents of globalization, who point to the boon that results from the trade in goods and services between countries, argue that global integration increases average income within countries, and also reduces inequality.

The antecedent for this view is typically attributed to 19th century British economist David Ricardo, who came up with the notion of 'comparative advantage' between countries. Witnessing firsthand the benefits of trade as a result of industrialization and cheap transportation (steamships and railways), Ricardo recommended that nations concentrate solely on those industries in which they are more competitive relative to other nations, and trade with other countries for all other products. Industry specialization and international trade, theorized Ricardo, always make countries better off.

Looking at the current wave of globalization, Nobel Laureate Eric Maskin of Harvard University arrives at a different conclusion. Maskin theorizes that while average income has been rising as a result of more trade and global production, so has inequality within countries.

How does one reconcile the visible benefits of globalization with the apparent downside?

8. With the Dollar as the World's Reserve Currency, Globalization Leads to Huge US Balance of Trade Deficits and Other Imbalances

With increased globalization and the rising price of oil since 2002, the US trade deficit has soared. The cumulative US deficit for the period 1980 through 2011 is $8.6 trillion. By the end of 2012, the cumulative deficit since 1980 is probably a little over 9 trillion.

A major reason for the large US trade deficit is the fact that the US dollar is the world's "reserve currency." While the mechanism is too complicated to explain here, the result is that the US can run deficits year after year, and the rest of the world will take their surpluses, and use it to buy US debt. With this arrangement, the rest of the world funds the United States' continued overspending.

> The answer, says Maskin, lies in contrasting the benefits to an economy as a whole against the negative effects on a certain segment of workers.
>
> "The right thing to do is not to try to stop globalization - that would be foolish -because globalization certainly does increase average income in all countries," says Maskin.
>
> "Rather, what we want to do," says Maskin, who confesses admiration for Ricardo's insights, "is allow the low skilled workers of the world to share in the fruits of globalization."
>
> How exactly does this happen?
>
> Maskin doesn't have an easy solution, but proposes a path of raising skill levels by offering job training to low-skilled workers so they can match better with international opportunities.
>
> Even if this were to be adopted as the most expedient way to tackle the challenge, a question that vexes Maskin even more is 'who is willing to pay to improve the skills of these workers?' The workers themselves can't afford to, says Maskin, and companies in need of more labor won't want to either, because that will eventually lead to a demand for higher wages.
>
> The most viable option, argues Maskin, is for third parties like governments, multilateral institutions, NGOs and private foundations to step in.
>
> *"Theorist Eric Maskin: Globalization Is Increasing Inequality," by Nahuel Berger, The World Bank Group, June 23, 2014.*

It is fairly clear the system was not put together with the thought that it would work in a fully globalized world—it simply leads to too great an advantage for the United States relative to other countries. Erik Townsend recently wrote an article called Why Peak Oil Threatens the International Monetary System, in which he talks about the possibility of high oil prices bringing an end to the current arrangement.

At this point, high oil prices together with globalization have led to huge US deficit spending since 2008. This has occurred partly because a smaller portion of the population is working (and thus paying taxes), and partly because US spending for unemployment benefits and stimulus has risen. The result is a mismatch between government income and spending.

Thanks to the mismatch described in the last paragraph, the federal deficit in recent years has been far greater than the balance of payment deficit. As a result, some other source of funding for the additional US debt has been needed, in addition to what is provided by the reserve currency arrangement. The Federal Reserve has been using quantitative easing to buy up federal debt since late 2008. This has provided a buyer for additional debt and also keeps US interest rates low (hoping to attract some investment back to the US, and keeping US debt payments affordable). The current situation is unsustainable, however. Continued overspending and printing money to pay debt is not a long-term solution to huge imbalances among countries and lack of cheap oil–situations that do not "go away" by themselves.

9. Globalization Tends to Move Taxation away from Corporations, and Onto Individual Citizens

Corporations have the ability to move to locations where the tax rate is lowest. Individual citizens have much less ability to make such a change. Also, with today's lack of jobs, each community competes with other communities with respect to how many tax breaks it can give to prospective employers. When we look at the breakdown of US tax receipts (federal, state, and local combined) this is what we find: The only portion that is entirely from corporations is corporate income taxes. This has clearly shrunk by more than half. Part of the excise, sales, and property tax [receipts category] is also from corporations, since truckers also pay excise tax on fuel they purchase, and businesses usually pay property taxes. It is clear, though, that the portion of revenue coming from personal income taxes and Social Security and Medicare funding has been rising.

I showed that high oil prices seem to lead to depressed US wages in my post, The Connection of Depressed Wages to High Oil Prices and Limits to Growth (https://ourfiniteworld.com/2013/02/14/the-connection-of-depressed-wages-to-high-oil-prices-and-limits-to-growth/). If wages are low at the same time that wage-earners are being asked to shoulder an increasing share of rising government costs, this creates a mismatch that wage-earners are not really able to handle.

10. Globalization Sets Up a Currency "Race to The Bottom," with Each Country Trying to Get an Export Advantage by Dropping the Value of Its Currency

Because of the competitive nature of the world economy, each country needs to sell its goods and services at as low a price as possible. This can be done in various ways–pay its workers lower wages; allow more pollution; use cheaper more polluting fuels; or debase the currency by quantitative easing (also known as "printing money,") in the hope that this will produce inflation and lower the value of the currency relative to other currencies.

There is no way this race to the bottom can end well. Prices of imports become very high in a debased currency–this becomes a problem. In addition, the supply of money is increasingly out of balance with real goods and services. This produces asset bubbles, such as artificially high stock market prices, and artificially high bond prices (because the interest rates on bonds are so low). These assets bubbles lead to investment crashes. Also, if the printing ever stops (and perhaps even if it doesn't), interest rates will rise, greatly raising cost to governments, corporations, and individual citizens.

11. Globalization Encourages Dependence on Other Countries for Essential Goods and Services

With globalization, goods can often be obtained cheaply from elsewhere. A country may come to believe that there is no point in producing its own food or clothing. It becomes easy to depend on imports and specialize in something like financial services or high-priced medical care–services that are not as oil-dependent.

As long as the system stays together, this arrangement works, more or less. However, if the built-in instabilities in the system become too great, and the system stops working, there is suddenly a very large problem. Even if the dependence is not on food, but is instead on computers and replacement parts for machinery, there can still be a big problem if imports are interrupted.

12. Globalization Ties Countries Together, So That if One Country Collapses, the Collapse Is Likely to Ripple Through the System, Pulling Many Other Countries with It

History includes many examples of civilizations that started from a small base, gradually grew to over-utilize their resource base, and then collapsed. We are now dealing with a world situation which is not too different. The big difference this time is that a large number of countries is involved, and these countries are increasingly interdependent. In my post 2013: Beginning of Long-Term Recession (https://ourfiniteworld.com/2013/01/06/2013-beginning-of-long-term-recession/), I showed that there are significant parallels between financial dislocations now happening in the United States and the types of changes which happened in other societies, prior to collapse. My analysis was based on the model of collapse developed in the book *Secular Cycles* by Peter Turchin and Sergey Nefedov.

It is not just the United States that is in perilous financial condition. Many European countries and Japan are in similarly poor condition. The failure of one country has the potential to pull many others down, and with it much of the system. The only countries that remain safe are the ones that have not grown to depend on globalization–which is probably not many today–perhaps landlocked countries of Africa.

In the past, when one area collapsed, there was less interdependence. When one area collapsed, it was possible to let cropland "rest" and deforested areas regrow. With regeneration, and perhaps new technology, it was possible for a new civilization to grow in the same area later. If we are dealing with a world-wide collapse, it will be much more difficult to follow this model.

VIEWPOINT 2

Emerging Multinationals Are Embracing Social Responsibility

Wharton School of the University of Pennsylvania

While some believe that corporations that make efforts to adjust their business practices to be more environmentally responsible should be credited, in the following viewpoint authors from the Wharton School of the University of Pennsylvania spotlight the ways many newer multinational corporations are embracing not just environmental responsibility, but social responsibility as well. This viewpoint appeared on the Knowledge@Wharton website, the online business analysis journal of the Wharton School, the business school of the University of Pennsylvania.

As you read, consider the following questions:

1. Why, according to this viewpoint, are large companies embracing policies that have a positive social impact?
2. Why is a commitment to corporate social responsibility (CSR) more challenging for companies in developing nations?
3. What are the advantages to companies of embracing CSR, according to this viewpoint?

Earlier this year, *Forbes* reported that New York-based natural foods company KIND Snacks, in its first ten years, has grown from zero to over 450 million units sold. Its now-familiar rainbow-

"How Emerging Multinationals Are Embracing Social Responsibility," Wharton School of the University of Pennsylvania, November 12, 2015. Reprinted by permission.

wrapped bars can now be found in over 150,000 retail stores. According to the article, founder and CEO Daniel Lubetzky's focus is to "make profit and make a difference ... achieve mass distribution and make his products healthy."

An example of "doing good and doing well"—or corporate social responsibility (CSR)—KIND is far from alone in its approach. Companies from startups to huge conglomerates are increasingly incorporating social and environmental initiatives into their strategies. Microsoft partners with the nonprofit NETHope to create IT apprenticeships in Kenya. The Disney Company is providing $3 million in conservation grants this year to protect wildlife. Gap Inc. has a program that teaches health awareness and literacy to women garment workers in Cambodia and India. JPMorgan Chase has The Fellowship Initiative, a program designed to help American young men of color achieve academic and professional success. Mattel is committed to using sustainably sourced paper and wood fiber in its packaging and products.

Mounting and sustaining social initiatives takes time, talent and resources. But increasingly, it is what investors, customers, employees and other stakeholders have come to expect and demand. Millennials—industry's new and future customers—cast a particularly keen eye on companies' commitment to social impact.

But is this phenomenon limited to American and European companies? What about emerging multinational firms from developing nations, fighting for survival and success in the global economy: Are they paying attention to CSR? Can they afford to? Can they afford not to?

Electric Cars, Cosmetics and More

There are some high-profile examples of emerging multinational companies engaged in socially or environmentally impactful activities. Chinese battery maker BYD brought out the first mass-market electric plug-in car in 2008, and earned the #1 spot on this year's Bloomberg *Businessweek* top 100 tech list. Despite a rocky entry into the U.S. market, it has built more than 1,000 electric buses and sold them in Asia, South America and Europe. In India, Suzlon Energy contributes to renewable energy as a major wind turbine manufacturer, operating on six continents.

And Natura Cosmeticos, one of Brazil's top cosmetics manufacturers, focuses on sustainability and social responsibility, serving as a founding member of the Union for Ethical BioTrade which promotes biodiversity conservation. According to Mauro Guillen and Esteban Garcia-Canal in their 2013 book *Emerging Markets Rule*, Natura uses only natural ingredients in its formulas, and has forged alliances with indigenous Amazon Basin communities to source herbal raw materials.

Tarun Khanna, a professor at Harvard Business School, points to India's Tata Group—one of India's largest conglomerates with revenues of $108.8 billion—as a company "long renowned for its commitment to social purpose." Greenbiz recently wrote, "In India, family-owned enterprises like the Tata Group occupy a place in citizen's hearts and minds that is not easily shifted. They are viewed as the 'go to'… to build schools and other social institutions, and fulfilling these social needs guarantees these companies' license to operate."

Khanna believes that emerging multinationals need to be even more attuned to social purpose than Western companies. "The way I think about it is that often in developing countries, the state fails to provide the public good. Ultimately, some societal actor has to step in at least partly, within the realm of private possibility, and well-run private sector entities are often the only game in town Twitter ."

Doing the Right Thing the Right Way

Wharton professor of management Witold Henisz sees a number of solid business reasons for any company to engage in social impact initiatives. But he cautions that CSR should be designed to address the concerns of stakeholders, not just "giving money to the symphony or something your stakeholders don't [necessarily] really care about…. The better CSR programs, either in emerging multinationals or developed-country multinationals ... are not just philanthropy, they're strategic."

He points to the CSR programs of big soda companies such as Coke and Pepsi, which are often focused on issues such as obesity, and water usage in developing nations, as good strategies. "These are programs addressing issues that people are concerned about with those companies. By addressing them, they reduce the likelihood of protest, they reduce the likelihood of aggressive regulation, and they build relations with stakeholders who could otherwise be attacking them."

Henisz labels as a "win-win-win" an ongoing project by Coke in which the company is investing in numerous small African mango plantations. "It's helping small farmers in Africa; it's getting them to think really well of Coca-Cola because Coca-Cola's helping them grow their livelihoods; but it's also creating a much bigger stock of mangos [for] Coke to create a mango-based beverage globally." The ultimate metric of CSR success is whether it is driving shareholder value and long-term sustainable performance, he says.

Winning Hearts and Minds

When it comes to social impact, Henisz sees some differences between developed-world firms and emerging multinationals. "In the West, in the developed countries, more companies have kind of been dragged into this and now realize the benefits. They're all going on a similar journey together." Whereas emerging markets display "much more polarized strategies": one sees "companies that embrace it from the beginning ... and companies that are reluctant or don't even see the value of it."

He identifies Chinese companies in particular as slow to adopt socially purposeful activities overseas because of their own political system. "Unfortunately, some of the Chinese oil and mining companies I run into in Africa where I do a lot of work [say,] 'Well, the government should take care of that.' Because in China, the government does take care of that." Social development in China is the Communist Party's responsibility, says Henisz, and businesses do not get involved. Only after "a lot of protests against them for not being more responsible, for not doing the same kinds of things that Western companies are doing," Chinese multinationals have begun to build up their CSR.

In other cases, says Henisz, an emerging multinational's attitude toward social purpose may stem from the way it achieved its original business success. It might have had to "survive in a very difficult, fraught environment" and so might be more inclined toward social responsibility. On the other hand, there are companies that have succeeded because "they're an offshoot of the government, related to the president, [or] they paid bribes, or they took advantage of a gap in the market and built up a monopoly." Those companies don't think at all about CSR, says Henisz, "because they got where they were by being ruthless and well-connected."

As an example of the former—an emerging multinational very much oriented toward CSR—Henisz cites Odebrecht, a Brazilian conglomerate with a large construction subsidiary. He says that Odebrecht nearly went bankrupt at its founding, but the CEO reached out to suppliers and buyers asking them to extend financing. The company survived the crisis, "and as a result, [the CEO has] always had this really strong relationship with his stakeholders—with the people in the supply chain and also the people all around his facilities." The company does business in Africa where, Henisz says, "they're involved not just in the big construction projects, but in really trying to win the hearts and minds of the people."

For example, while competing for a large construction contract in Luanda, Angola, Odebrecht took the unusual step of taking on a street-sweeping contract. Henisz explains that this gave them some very visible PR: The employees, sporting orange Odebrecht vests, were seen tackling one of downtown Luanda's fundamental problems by cleaning up its streets. Another bonus was that many of these individuals, who would eventually work on Odebrecht's construction sites, were acquiring basic job skills such as following processes and arriving on time. While acknowledging that Odebrecht "has been a little tarred in a corruption scandal recently," Henisz says, "I still think, when I see their operations overseas, that they know what it means to come from a poor country; they know what the basic problems are; they know how to make a connection to the people as a result."

By contrast, a multinational that ignores CSR might look something like Brazil's EBX Group, according to Henisz. Its chairman, the mining, oil and gas magnate Eike Batista, had a net worth of $30 billion in 2012, but his wealth sank to $200 million due to debts and his company's plummeting stock prices. His fall from grace and his trial for insider trading were widely reported in the business press. "His mines had nothing in terms of socially responsible behavior," Henisz comments. "His company wasn't based on success in the community. It was based on kind of moving envelopes of cash around and convincing people that he had connections." EBX is now bankrupt, Henisz points out.

Social Purpose in Health Care

An emerging multinational in the health care space, and one very much focused on social purpose, is Narayana Hrudayalaya Private Ltd. in India. The for-profit company, founded in 2000 and now with 56 facilities in India and one in the Cayman Islands, was started by heart surgeon Devi Shetty to provide low-cost or free cardiac procedures to the poor and underserved. It has since expanded to treat other medical conditions as well.

Harvard's Khanna, who has done pro bono work and research for the organization for over a decade, comments, "What's neat about it is that it's now the lowest-cost heart surgery (for example for coronary artery bypass graft, and many other procedures) in the world. Think more than 90% cheaper than in the US."

Shetty introduced a unique business model, drawing on economies of scale, which has allowed Narayana Health to help indigent patients while remaining profitable. Khanna notes that the Wall Street Journal a few years ago dubbed Shetty "the Henry Ford of heart surgery" He adds: "Though I think better than to use a comparison with Ford and its standardized mass production system [would be a comparison] with Toyota and its famed learning approach to describe what Shetty has pulled off."

No patient is ever turned away from Narayana, notes Khanna. Patients who cannot pay are treated at no cost or through charity efforts that the hospital chain coordinates. "So, it has to be efficient enough to both turn a profit and to make money available for this social mission. Very cool."

Of emerging multinationals and social purpose, Khanna notes that one of the "underappreciated benefits of being attuned to social impact" is that it puts you "on the cutting edge of many of society's most pressing issues." A well-run firm and a motivated entrepreneur can turn this to substantial advantage, he says.

Thomas Robertson, a former dean of the Wharton School and a professor of marketing, comments that while "obviously you have to keep your focus on profits or you won't meet any of your objectives," increasingly, business has moved from a shareholder model to the more encompassing stakeholder model. He sees increased recognition by industry of its responsibilities to employees, customers and the neighborhoods and regions in which it operates. "It's kind of hard to [just] walk away from that."

VIEWPOINT 3

Globalization Has Changed the Rules of the Game

Milan Babic, Eelke Heemskerk, and Jan Fichtner

In chapter one we read viewpoints saying that the power of multinational corporations had subverted democracy. In the following viewpoint Milan Babic, Eelke Heemskerk and Jan Fichtner explain how state power has changed to allow for the interests and concerns of large, powerful corporations. Milan Babic, Eelke Heemskerk, and Jan Fichtner are political science scholars at the University of Amsterdam in The Netherlands.

As you read, consider the following questions:

1. Why would the president of the United States consult with the president of a technology company before making a decision about trade policies, according to this viewpoint? What does this say about corporate power?
2. The top three or four economies are still nation states (or the Eurozone), but many corporations are larger than most nations. According to this viewpoint, what does that mean for international relations?
3. How, according to the authors, might the new role of corporations lead to a revival of global rivalries?

"Who Is More Powerful—States or Corporations?" by Milan Babic, Eelke Heemskerk and Jan Fichtner, The Conversation, July 11, 2018. https://theconversation.com/who-is-more-powerful-states-or-corporations-99616. Licensed under CC BY ND 4.0.

Causes and Effects of Global Corporate Dominance

Who holds the power in international politics? Most people would probably say it's the largest states in the global system. The current landscape of international relations seems to affirm this intuition: new Russian geopolitics, "America First" and Chinese state-led global expansion, among others, seem to put state power back in charge after decades of globalisation.

Yet multinationals like Apple and Starbucks still wield phenomenal power. They oversee huge supply chains, sell products all over the world, and help mould international politics to their interests. In some respects, multinationals have governments at their beck and call—witness their consistent success at dodging tax payments. So when it comes to international politics, are states really calling the shots?

We compare states and corporations based on how deep their pockets are. The following table ranks the 100 largest corporations and countries on the basis of their revenues in 2016. Revenues in the case of states is mainly collected taxes.

States occupy the top rankings, with the US first followed by China and Japan (the eurozone ranks first with more than US$5,600 billion if we treat it as a single political entity). But plenty of corporations are on par with some of the largest economies in the world: Walmart exceeds Spain and Australia, for example. Of the top 100 revenue generators, our ranking shows 71 are corporations.

Notice also that the top ranked corporations follow the same nationality-order as states: America's Walmart is followed by three Chinese firms. There are already 14 Chinese firms in the top 100, though the US has 27.

Our comparison is necessarily crude, but suggests that besides the very largest states, the economic power of corporations and states is essentially on par. This prompted us to try and rethink corporate power in international politics in a recent paper. We argued that globalisation has brought about a global structure in which state power is not the exclusive governing principle anymore.

Just think about the private and public power of global giants like Google or Apple. When Donald Trump recently met Apple chief executive Tim Cook to discuss how a trade war with China would affect Apple's interests, it demonstrated that the leading multinationals are political actors, not bystanders.

There always existed big and powerful global corporations – the Dutch East India Company dominated European trade in the 1600s and 1700s, for instance. But global corporations' current power position vis-à-vis other actors is unprecedented in terms of sheer size and volume.

How Global Power Works

State power did not disappear with globalisation, but it transformed. It now competes with corporations for influence and political power. States use corporations and vice versa, as the following two examples illustrate: offshore finance and transnational state-owned enterprises.

To start with offshore finance, global corporations use different jurisdictions to avoid being taxed or regulated in their home country. Lost taxes due to profit shifting could be as high as US$500 billion globally. When states position themselves as tax havens, they undermine the ability of "onshore" states to tax corporations and wealthy individuals – a cornerstone of state power.

Besides tax havens, numerous EU governments have become notorious for offering "sweetheart deals" that reduce the tax burden for specific multinationals to an astonishing extent. Also, our CORPNET research group at the University of Amsterdam recently identified five countries who play an important additional role in facilitating tax avoidance: the UK, the Netherlands, Switzerland, Ireland and Singapore. Each enables multinationals to shift investments at minimum cost between tax havens and onshore states.

Turning to our second example, states have grown as global corporate owners in recent years. They now control almost one quarter of the Fortune Global 500. By investing in state-owned enterprises beyond their borders, states gain strategic leverage vis-à-vis other states or actors—Russia's gas pipeline holdings via

Gazprom in eastern Europe are a good example. This has led some observers to diagnose a potential transformation of the liberal world order through "state capitalism".

China (CN) controls over 1,000 TSOEs, including the likes of Sinopec and ICBC China. Countries like France (FR) and Germany (DE) are also prominent owners, but their connections to China highlight that they are targets of TSOE investment, too.

It starts to become apparent that international relations are anything but a one-sided story of either state or corporate power. Globalisation has changed the rules of the game, empowering corporations but bringing back state power through new transnational state-corporate relations. International relations has become a giant three-dimensional chess game with states and corporations as intertwined actors.

This transformation of the global environment is probably here to stay and even accelerate. Washington recently blocked the large Chinese telecommunications manufacturer ZTE from access to critical American suppliers, for example. It did this to gain advantage in trade negotiations with Beijing. The Chinese Sovereign Wealth Fund then withdrew its longstanding investment in the American Blackstone Group following Trump's push for economic sanctions on China.

We live in an era where the interplay between state and corporate power shapes the reality of international relations more than ever. In combination with the current nationalist and protectionist backlash in large parts of the world, this may yet lead to a revival of global rivalries: states using corporations to achieve geopolitical goals in an increasingly hostile environment, and powerful corporations perhaps using more aggressive strategies to extract profits in response. If this is where we're heading, it could have a lasting impact on the world order.

Viewpoint 4

In the United States a Free Media Is Essential to Democracy, but Corporate Media Really Is "the Enemy of the People"

Paul Street

Corporations that manufacture or sell goods are not the only big businesses that have international reach. In the following excerpted viewpoint Paul Street makes the case for why the consolidation of media in the hands of a few large corporations is antithetical to democracy and the good of the citizenry. Paul Street is an independent journalist, author, and historian.

As you read, consider the following questions:

1. What sort of false image does the corporate media sell to the American public, according to the author?
2. How does this viewpoint define "idiocy," and what is the advantage of corporate media in promoting that type of idiocy?
3. This viewpoint ends on a positive note. What "struggle" does the author say "lives on"?

I detest the malignantly racist, sexist, narcissistic, and authoritarian pathological liar and bully Donald Trump on many different levels, and I share none of his sick world view, but the corporate

"Corporate Media: The Enemy of the People," by Paul Street, Counter Punch, August 17, 2018. Reprinted by permission.

media really is, well (to use Trump's recurrent phrase), "the enemy of the people."

Here below is an essay I first published (on the venerable radical Website ZNet) in the late summer of 2015. […] It was written from a Marxist and international socialist and anti-imperialist perspective and not at all from a Trumpian, white-nationalist standpoint.

[…]

"Homeland" Distortion

Consistent with its possession as a leading and money-making asset of the nation's wealthy elite, the United States corporate and commercial mass media is a bastion of power-serving propaganda and deadening twaddle designed to keep the U.S. citizenry subordinated to capital and the imperial U.S. state. It regularly portrays the United States as a great model of democracy and equality. It sells a false image of the U.S. as a society where the rich enjoy opulence because of hard and honest work and where the poor are poor because of their laziness and irresponsibility. The nightly television news broadcasts and television police and law and order dramas are obsessed with violent crime in the nation's Black ghettoes and Latino barrios, but they never talk about the extreme poverty, the absence of opportunity imposed on those neighborhoods by the interrelated forces of institutional racism, capital flight, mass structural unemployment, under-funded schools, and mass incarceration. The nightly television weather reports tells U.S. citizens of ever new record high temperatures and related forms of extreme weather but never relate these remarkable meteorological developments to anthropogenic climate change.

The dominant corporate U.S. media routinely exaggerates the degree of difference and choice between the candidates run by the nation's two corporate-dominated political organizations, the Democrats and the Republicans. It never notes that the two reigning parties agree about far more than they differ on, particularly when it comes to fundamental and related matters of business class power and American Empire. It shows U.S. protestors engaged in angry confrontations with police and highlights isolated examples of protestor violence but it downplays peaceful protest and never pays serious attention to the important societal and policy issues that have sparked protest or to the demands and recommendations advanced by protest movements.

[…]

More than Entertainment

The U.S. corporate media's propagandistic service to the nation's reigning and interrelated structures of Empire and inequality is hardly limited to its news and public affairs wings. Equally if not more significant in that regard is that media's vast "entertainment" sector, which is loaded with political and ideological content but was completely ignored in Herman and Chomsky's groundbreaking Manufacturing Consent.[3] One example is the Hollywood movie "Zero Dark Thirty," a 2012 "action thriller" that dramatized the United States' search for Osama bin-Laden after the September 11, 2001 jetliner attacks. The film received critical acclaim and was a box office-smash. It was also a masterpiece of pro-military, pro-CIA propaganda, skillfully portraying U.S. torture practices "as a dirty, ugly business that is necessary to protect America" (Glenn Greenwald[4]) and deleting the moral debate that erupted over the CIA's "enhanced interrogation techniques." Under the guise of a neutral, documentary-like façade, *Zero Dark Thirty* normalized and endorsed torture in ways that were all the more effective because of its understated, detached, and "objective" veneer. The film also marked a distressing new frontier in U.S. military-"embedded" filmmaking whereby the movie-makers receive technical and logistical support from the Pentagon in return for producing elaborate public relations on the military's behalf.

The 2014–15 Hollywood blockbuster *American Sniper* is another example. The film's audiences is supposed to marvel at the supposedly noble feats, sacrifice, and heroism of Chris Kyle, a rugged, militantly patriotic, and Christian-fundamentalist Navy SEALS sniper who participated in the U.S. invasion of Iraq to fight "evil" and to avenge the al Qaeda jetliner attacks of September 11, 2001. Kyle killed 160 Iraqis over four tours of "duty" in "Operational Iraqi Freedom." Viewers are never told that the Iraqi government had nothing to do with the 9/11 attacks or al Qaeda or that the U.S. invasion was one of the most egregiously criminal and brazenly imperial and mass-murderous acts in the history of international violence. Like Zero Dark Thirty's apologists, American Sniper's defenders claim that the film takes a neutral perspective of "pure storytelling," with no ideological bias. In reality, the movie is filled with racist and imperial distortions, functioning as flat-out war propaganda.[5]

[…]

Manufacturing Idiocy

Seen broadly in its many-sided and multiply delivered reality, U.S. corporate media's dark, power-serving mission actually goes further than the manufacture of consent. A deeper goal is the manufacture of mass idiocy, with "idiocy" understood in the original Greek and Athenian sense not of stupidity but of childish selfishness and willful indifference to public affairs and concerns. (An "idiot" in Athenian democracy was characterized by self-centeredness and concerned almost exclusively with private instead of public affairs.).

[…]

In U.S. movies, television sit-coms, television dramas, television reality-shows, commercials, state Lottery advertisements, and video games, the ideal-type U.S. citizen is an idiot in this classic sense: a person who cares about little more than his or her own well-being, consumption, and status. This noble American idiot is blissfully indifferent to the terrible prices paid by others for the maintenance of reigning and interrelated oppressions structures at home and abroad.

A pervasive theme in this media culture is the notion that people at the bottom of the nation's steep and interrelated socioeconomic and racial pyramids are the "personally irresponsible" and culturally flawed makers of their own fate. The mass U.S. media's version of Athenian idiocy "can imagine," in the words of the prolific Left U.S. cultural theorist Henry Giroux "public issues only as private concerns." It works to "erase the social from the language of public life so as to reduce" questions of racial and socioeconomic disparity to "private issues of …individual character and cultural depravity. Consistent with "the central neoliberal tenet that all problems are private rather than social in nature," it portrays the only barriers to equality and meaningful democratic participation as "a lack of principled self-help and moral responsibility" and bad personal choices by the oppressed. Government efforts to meaningfully address and ameliorate (not to mention abolish) societal disparities of race, class, gender, ethnicity, nationality and the like are portrayed as futile, counterproductive, naïve, and dangerous.[8]

[…]

Like the U.S. ruling class that owns it, the purportedly anti-government corporate media isn't really opposed to government as such. It's opposed to what the French sociologist Pierre Bourdieu called "the left hand of the state"—the parts of the public sector that serve the social and democratic needs of the non-affluent majority. It celebrates and otherwise advances the "right hand of the state"[9]: the portions of government that serve the opulent minority, dole out punishment for the poor, and attacks those perceived as nefariously resisting the corporate and imperial order at home and abroad. Police officers, prosecutors, military personnel, and other government authorities who represent the "right hand of the state" are heroes and role models in this media. Public defenders, other defense attorneys, civil libertarians, racial justice activists, union leaders, antiwar protesters and the like are presented at best as naïve and irritating "do-gooders" and at worst as coddlers and even agents of evil.

The generation of mass idiocy in the more commonly understood sense of sheer stupidity is also a central part of U.S. "mainstream" media's mission. Nowhere is this more clearly evident than in the constant barrage of rapid-fire advertisements that floods U.S. corporate media. As the American cultural critic Neil Postman noted thirty years ago, the modern U.S. television commercial is the antithesis of the rational economic consideration that early Western champions of the profits system claimed to be the enlightened essence of capitalism. "Its principal theorists, even its most prominent practitioners," Postman noted, "believed capitalism to be based on the idea that both buyer and seller are sufficiently mature, well-informed, and reasonable to engage in transactions of mutual self-interest." Commercials make "hash" out of this idea. They are dedicated to persuading consumers with wholly irrational claims. They rely not on the reasoned presentation of evidence and logical argument but on suggestive emotionalism, infantilizing manipulation, and evocative, rapid-fire imagery.[10]

The same techniques poison U.S. electoral politics. Investment in deceptive and manipulative campaign commercials commonly determines success or failure in mass-marketed election contests between business-beholden candidates that are sold to the audience/electorate like brands of toothpaste and deodorant.

[…]

These commercials assault citizens' capacity for sustained mental focus and rational deliberation nearly sixteen minutes of every hour on cable television, with 44 percent of the individual ads now running for just 15 seconds. This is a factor in the United States' long-bemoaned epidemic of "Attention Deficit Disorder."

The Dominance of Global Corporations

[...]

Explaining "Mainstream" Media Corporate Ownership

There's nothing surprising about the fact that the United States' supposedly "free" and "independent" media functions as a means of mass indoctrination for the nation's economic and imperial elite. The first and most important explanation for this harsh reality is concentrated private ownership—the fundamental fact that that media is owned primarily by giant corporations representing wealthy interests who are deeply invested in U.S. capitalism and Empire. Visitors to the U.S. should not be fooled by the large number and types of channels and stations on a typical U.S. car radio or television set or by the large number and types of magazines and books on display at a typical Barnes & Noble bookstore. Currently in the U.S., just six massive and global corporations—Comcast, Viacom, Time Warner, CBS, The News Corporation and Disney—together control more than 90 percent of the nation's print and electronic media, including cable television, airwaves television, radio, newspapers, movies, video games, book publishing, comic books, and more. Three decades ago, 50 corporations controlled the same amount of U.S. media.

[...]

As the nation's media becomes concentrated into fewer corporate hands, media personnel become ever more insecure in their jobs because they have fewer firms to whom to sell their skills. That makes them even less willing than they might have been before to go outside official sources, to question the official line, and to tell the truth about current events and the context in which they occur.

Advertisers

A second explanation is the power of advertisers. U.S. media managers are naturally reluctant to publish or broadcast material that might offend the large corporations that pay for broadcasting by purchasing advertisements.

[…]

At the same time, both U.S. corporate media managers and the advertisers who supply revenue for their salaries are hesitant to produce content that might alienate the affluent people who count for an ever rising share of consumer purchases in the U.S. It is naturally those with the most purchasing power who are naturally most targeted by advertisers.

Government Policy

[…] The U.S. corporate media is hardly a "natural" outcome of a "free market." It's the result of government protections and subsidies that grant enormous "competitive" advantages to the biggest and most politically/plutocratically influential media firms. Under the terms of the 1934 Communications Act and the 1996 Telecommunications Act, commercial, for-profit broadcasters have almost completely free rein over the nation's airwaves and cable lines. There is no substantive segment of the broadcast spectrum set aside for truly public interest and genuinely democratic, popular not-for profit media and the official "public" broadcasting networks are thoroughly captive to corporate interests and to right-wing politicians who take giant campaign contributions from corporate interests. Much of the 1996 bill was written by lobbyists working for the nations' leading media firms.[13]

[…]

"The Internet Will Save Us"

[…] In the U.S. as elsewhere, those with access to the Internet and the time and energy to use it meaningfully can find a remarkable breadth and depth of information and trenchant Left analysis at various online sites. The Internet also broadens U.S. citizens and activists' access to media networks beyond the U.S.—to elite sources that are much less beholden of course to U.S. propaganda and ideology. At the same time, the Internet and digital telephony

The Dominance of Global Corporations

networks have at times shown themselves to be effective grassroots organizing tools for progressive U.S. activists.

Still, the democratic and progressive impact of the Internet in the U.S. is easily exaggerated. Left and other progressive online outlets lack anything close to the financial, technical, and organizational and human resources of the corporate news media, which has its own sophisticated Internet.

[…]

Along the way, the notion of a great "democratizing," Wild West" and "free market" Internet has proved politically useful for the corporate media giants. The regularly trumpet the great Internet myth to claim that the U.S. public and regulators don't need to worry about corporate media power and to justify their demands for more government subsidy and protection. At the same time, finally, we know from the revelations of Edward Snowden, Glenn Greenwald and others that the nation's leading digital and Internet-based e-mail (Google and Yahoo), telephony (e.g. Verizon), and "social network" (Facebook above all) corporations have collaborated with the National Security Agency and with the nation's local, state, and federal police in the surveillance of U.S. citizens' and activists' private communications.[17]

[…]

A False Paradox

The propagandistic and power-serving mission and nature of dominant U.S, corporate mass media might seem ironic and even paradoxical in light of the United States' strong free speech and democratic traditions. In fact, as Carey and Chomsky have noted, the former makes perfect sense in light of the latter. In nations where popular expression and dissent is routinely crushed with violent repression, elites have little incentive to shape popular perceptions in accord with elite interests. The population is controlled primarily through physical coercion. In societies where it is not generally considered legitimate to put down popular expression with the iron heel of armed force and where dissenting opinion is granted a significant measure of freedom of expression, elites are heavily and dangerously incentivized to seek to manufacture mass popular consent and idiocy. The danger is deepened by the United States' status as the pioneer in the development of mass consumer capitalism, advertising, film, and television. Thanks to that history, corporate America has long stood in the global vanguard when it comes to developing the technologies, methods, art, and science of mass persuasion and thought control.[20]

[…]

Its success is easily exaggerated, however. To everyday Americans' credit, corporate media has never been fully successful in stamping out popular resistance and winning over the hearts and minds of the U.S. populace. A recent Pew Research poll showed that U.S. "millennials" (young adults 18-29 years old) have a more favorable response to the word "socialism" than to "capitalism"—a remarkable finding on the limits of corporate media and other forms of elite ideological power in the U.S. […] The U.S. elite is no more successful in its utopian (or dystopian) quest to control every American heart and mind than it is in its equally impossible ambition of managing events across a complex planet from the banks of the Potomac River in Washington D.C. The struggle for popular self-determination, democracy, justice, and equality lives on despite the influence of corporate media.

Notes

3. For elaboration, see Paul Street, "More Than Entertainment," Monthly Review, Vol. 51, No. 9 (February 2000); Paul Street, "Beyond Manufacturing Consent," TeleSur English, March 27, 2015,; Paul Street. "Reflections on a Forgotten Book: Herbert Schiller's The Mind Managers (1973)," ZNet(April 5, 2009),
4. Glen Greenwald, "Zero Dark Thirty: CIA Hagiography, Pernicious Propaganda," The Guardian (UK,). December 14, 2012.
5. For elaboration, see Paul Street, "Hollywood's Service to Empire," Counterpunch (February 20-22, 2015),
8. Henry A. Giroux, The Abandoned Generation: Democracy Beyond the Culture of Fear (New York: Palgrave-MacMillan, 2003); Henry A. Giroux, The Terror of Neoliberalism (Boulder, CO: Paradigm, 2004).
9. Pierre Bourdieu, Acts of Resistance (New York, NY: Free Press, 1998), 2, 24-44; John Pilger, The New Rulers of the World (London: Verso, 2002), 5, 116.

The Dominance of Global Corporations

10. Neil Postman, Amusing Ourselves to Death: Public Discourse in the Age of Show Business (New York: Penguin, 1983), 127-128; Noam Chomsky, Power Systems (New York: Metropolitan Books, 2013), 80.
13. For a richly researched historical treatment of U.S. media policy, see the following works by the United States' leading Left media policy critic and analyst Robert W. McChesney: Telecommunications, Mass Media, and Democracy: The Battle for the Control of U.S. Broadcasting, 1928-1933 (New York: Oxford University Press, 1994); Corporate Media and the Threat to Democracy (New York: Seven Stories, 1997); Rich Media, Poor Democracy: Communication Politics in Dubious Times (New York: New Press, 2000).
17. Essential here is Glenn Greenwald, No Place to Hide: Edward Snowden, the NSA, and the U.S. Surveillance State(New York: Metropolitan, 2014).
20. Carey, Taking the Risk Out of Democracy, 11-14, 133-139. Noam Chomsky, Deterring Democracy (New York: Hill and Wang, 1992), Chapter 12: "Force and Opinion," 351-406; Street, "Reflections on a Forgotten Book."

VIEWPOINT 5

The Rise of Global Corporate Power Is Increasing Inequality

Sarah Anderson and John Cavanagh

In the following viewpoint Sarah Anderson and John Cavanagh begin by pointing out the fact that a mere two hundred global corporations account for more than a quarter of the world's economic activity. The authors list ten alarming facts, then go on the explain how this situation is responsible not for global economic growth, but the growth of inequality. Sarah Anderson is director of the Global Economy Project at the Institute for Policy Studies. John Cavanagh has been Director of the Institute for Policy Studies since 1999.

As you read, consider the following questions:

1. What, according to this viewpoint, is the most alarming finding mentioned here?
2. What do the authors mean by the phrase "global apartheid"?
3. What, according to Anderson and Cavanagh, are the implications of the world's economic activity being consolidated in such a small percentage of corporations?

There are now 40,000 corporations in the world whose activities cross national boundaries; these firms ply overseas markets through some 250,000 foreign affiliates.[1] Yet, new calculations by the Institute for Policy Studies (IPS) indicate that the top 200 of

"Top 200: The Rise of Global Corporate Power," by Sarah Anderson and John Cavanagh, Global Policy Forum. Reprinted by permission.

these global firms account for an alarming and growing share of the world's economic activity.

Two hundred giant corporations, most of them larger than many national economies, now control well over a quarter of the world's economic activity. Philip Morris is larger than New Zealand, and it operates in 170 countries.[2] Instead of creating an integrated global village, these firms are weaving webs of production, consumption, and finance that bring economic benefits to, at most, a third of the world's people. Two-thirds of the world (the bottom 20 percent of the rich countries and the bottom 80 percent of the poor countries) are either left out, marginalized, or hurt by these webs of activity.

IPS has conducted detailed analyses of the changing nature of global corporate power for over a decade. This new report uncovers an alarming acceleration in corporate concentration in individual sectors and in the overall power of the largest corporations in the world, and new data on the job-destroying activities of large firms.

The most alarming finding is that as corporate concentration has risen, corporate profits have soared, yet workers and communities are getting a shrinking piece of the growing pie. Figures from Business Week chronicle the explosion of corporate profits and CEO pay between 1990 and 1995 in the face of stagnating workers wages. The newest State of Working America by the Economic Policy Institute also reinforces our findings: median family income fell over 1 percent a year between 1989 and 1994 after four decades of expansion.[3]

Top 10 Findings

1. Of the 100 largest economies in the world, 51 are corporations; only 49 are countries. Wal-Mart-the number 12 corporation-is bigger than 161 countries, including Israel, Poland, and Greece.[4] Mitsubishi is larger than the fourth most populous nation on earth: Indonesia. General Motors is bigger than Denmark. Ford is bigger than South Africa. Toyota is bigger than Norway.

Causes and Effects of Global Corporate Dominance

2. The combined sales of the world's Top 200 corporations are far greater than a quarter of the world's economic activity. Our calculations indicate that the Top 200's share of global economic activity has been growing rapidly over the past decade. In 1982, the Top 200 firms had sales that were the equivalent of 24.2 percent of the world's GDP. Today, that figure has grown to 28.3 percent of world GDP.

3. The Top 200 corporations' combined sales are bigger than the combined economies of all countries minus the biggest 9; that is they surpass the combined economies of 182 countries. At latest count, the world has 191 countries. If you subtract the GDP of the big nine economies: the United States, Japan, Germany, France, Italy, the United Kingdom, Brazil, Canada, and China, the combined GDP's of the other 182 countries is $6.9 trillion. The combined sales of the Top 200 corporations is $7.1 trillion.

4. The Top 200 have almost twice the economic clout of the poorest four-fifths of humanity. The world's economic income and wealth remain highly concentrated among the rich. Indeed, according to the United Nations, some 85 percent of the world's GDP is controlled by the richest fifth of humanity; only 15 percent is controlled by the poorest four-fifths.[5] Hence, the poorer 4.5 billion people in the world account for only $3.9 trillion dollars of economic activity; this is only a little over half the combined revenues of the Top 200's $7.1 trillion.

5. The Top 200 have been net job destroyers in recent years. Their combined global employment is only 18.8 million, which is less than a third of one percent of the world's people. The world has just over 5.6 billion people.[6] Of these, around 2.6 billion are in the workforce.[7] Hence, the Top 200 employ less than three-fourths of one percent of the world's workers. Of the world's top five employers, four are U.S. (General Motors, Wal-Mart, PepsiCo, and Ford), and one is German (Siemens). If one also includes the public sector in these calculations, the U.S. Postal Service is the world's biggest employer, at 870,160, roughly 160,000 more workers than GM's 709,000 workers.[8]

6. Not only are the world's largest corporations cutting workers, their CEOs often benefit financially from the job cuts. A total of 59 of the Global Top 200 are U.S. firms. Of these, 9 laid off at least 3,000 workers in 1995: AT&T, Boeing, Lockheed-Martin, BellSouth, Kmart, Chase Manhattan, GTE, Mobil, and Texaco. Even worse, the CEOs of these 9 made millions of dollars in the increased value of their stock options after announcing the layoffs. Indeed, on the day that the CEOs of these 9 firms announced the layoffs, the value of the stock options of their 9 CEOs rose $25,218,819.[9]

7. Japanese corporations have surpassed U.S. corporations in the ranking of the Top 200. Six of the top 10 firms are Japanese; only 3 are from the United States. Of the Top 200, the 58 Japanese firms account for almost 39 percent of total sales, while the U.S.'s 59 firms account for only 28 percent of total sales. The vast majority (186) of the Top 200 are headquartered in just 7 countries: Japan, the United States, Germany, France, the United Kingdom, the Netherlands, and Switzerland. South Korea and Brazil are the only developing countries to break into the Top 200.

8. Over half of the sales of the Top 200 are in just 5 economic sectors; and corporate concentration in these sectors is high. Half of the total sales of the Top 200 are in trading, automobiles, banking, retailing, and electronics. The concentrated economic power in these and other sectors is enormous.[10] In autos, the top five firms account for almost 60 percent of global sales. In electronics, the top five firms have garnered over half of global sales. And, the top five firms have over 30 percent of global sales in airlines, aerospace, steel, oil, personal computers, chemical, and the media.[11]

9. When General Motors trades with itself, is that free trade?: One-third of world trade is simply transactions among various units of the same corporation.[12] This figure has remained steady for the past few years, and is higher in certain countries.[13] Two-fifths of Japanese exports, for example, are intra-firm.[14] For manufacturing exports from Brazil, the figure is 44 percent.[15]

10. The Top 200 are creating a global economic apartheid, not a global village. The top eight telecommunications firms, for

example, have been expanding global sales rapidly, yet over nine-tenths of humanity remains without phones. Television ads for AT&T and GTE give the impression that the telecommunications giants are bringing the world closer together. And yet while the top eight firms in this sector enjoyed sales of $290 million in 1995, 90.1 percent of all people live in a household that is not connected to a telephone line.[16] Likewise in the financial sector, when banks boast of the new ease of global banking, they fail to mention the difficulties most of the world's people face in obtaining even a tiny loan. Close to 4.8 billion of the world's 5.6 billion people still live in countries where the average per capita gross national product is less than $1,000 a year; only a handful of these people have access to credit from transnational banks.[17] This is despite the fact that the 31 banks in the Top 200 have combined assets of $10.4 trillion and sales of more than $800 billion.[18]

Conclusions

These findings offer a clear picture of the rising inequalities in the United States and the world between those who benefit from expanding corporate activity and those who are being left behind. This inequality, fueled by accelerated corporate concentration, deserves to be a central issue in the political debates of this period. This report stands as a challenge to both major political parties to address growing inequalities and the economic forces behind them.

Notes

1. United Nations Conference on Trade and Development, World Investment Report 1995 (Geneva: UNCTAD, 1996).
2. See Richard J. Barnet and John Cavanagh, Global Dreams: Imperial Corporations and the New World Order (New York: Simon & Schuster, 1994).
3. Lawrence Mishel, Jared Bernstein, and John Schmitt, The State of Working America (Washington, D.C., 1996).
4. The number of countries in the world has been changing rapidly. At latest count, there were 191. There are 30 countries whose GDP is greater than Wal-Mart, and 161 whose GDP is smaller.
5. These figures are from an interview with a statistician at the United Nations Development Program.
6. According to the World Bank, the world had 5.601 people in 1994. World Bank, World Development Report 1996 (Washington, D.C.: World Bank, 1996), p. 195.

The Dominance of Global Corporations

7. The United Nations estimates that 47 percent of the world's population is in the workforce. See United Nations Development Program, Human Development Report, 1996 (New York: Oxford University Press, 1996), p. 194.
8. See Fortune, August 5, 1996, p. F-1.
9. See The Institute for Policy Studies, "CEOs Win, Workers Lose: How Wall Street Rewards Job Destroyers," April 24, 1996.
10. The figures in this section are from Morgan Stanley Capital International and the International Data Corporation, quoted in The Economist, March 27, 1993, p. Survey 17.
11. "A Game of Global Monopoly," The Economist, March 27, 1993, p.S17.
12. United Nations Conference on Trade and Development, World Investment Report 1995 (Geneva: UNCTAD, 1996).
13. In 1993, the United Nations calculated that of the $3.3 trillion in exports of goods and services in 1990, roughly $1.1 trillion was intra-firm trade (from UNCTC, E/C.10/1993/2, March 3, 1993, p. 8).
14. Dennis Encarnation, "A common evolution? A comparison of United States and Japanese transnational corporations," Transnational Corporations, UNCTC, February 1993.
15. Karl Sauvant, et. al, "Foreign direct investment and international migration," Transnational Corporations, UNCTC, February 1993, p. 43.
16. United Nations Development Program, Human Development Report 1996, p. 167.
17. World Bank, World Development Report 1996, p. 189; and United Nations Development Program, Human Development Report 1996, p. 145.
18. The bank sales are from Table 4; the assets are calculated by the authors from Forbes, April 22, 1996 and July 15, 1996.

VIEWPOINT 6

In the United Kingdom Recent Decisions on Parent Company Liability Cases Show the Need for Law Reform

William Meade

In the following viewpoint William Meade argues that the United Kingdom should reform laws regarding the liability of parent companies. The author contends that giant multinational corporations are often responsible for human rights and environmental abuses, but there are few legal consequences for these actions. The good news, he writes, is that there is a clear trend towards embedding the corporate responsibility to protect human rights into law. William Meade is Policy and Communications Officer at CORE Coalition, an organization that works to end corporate practices that harm people and the environment.

As you read, consider the following questions:

1. What did the ruling in Chandler v Cape hold?
2. Why do the Zambian villagers mentioned in the viewpoint have a slim chance of obtaining justice in their own country?
3. What does the 2017 French *devoir de vigilance* require?

"Recent Decisions in the UK On Parent Company Liability Cases Show the Need for Law Reform," by William Meade, Corporate Responsibility.org. Reprinted by permission.

The Dominance of Global Corporations

The UK is home to some of the largest multinational corporations in the world operating through integrated networks of subsidiary companies and complex supply chains. Through their global activities, UK companies are often involved in human rights and environmental abuses.

There have been important developments towards improved access to remedy in the UK for victims of overseas corporate related harm over the last 25 years, culminating in the 2012 Court of Appeal ruling in *Chandler v Cape* which held that, under certain circumstances, a parent company could owe a legal duty of care to employees of its subsidiaries. At present, however, there is no statutory regime in the UK for dealing with alleged violations of human rights by corporate actors.

This gap has become particularly apparent in the past twelve months as several major multinationals have succeeded in persuading the courts that they are not responsible for serious human rights abuses connected to their subsidiaries' operations.

In three parent company liability cases heard before the UK Court of Appeal—*Lungowe v. Vedanta*, *Okpabi v. Shell*, and *AAA v. Unilever*—companies have argued that their UK headquarters are a separate legal entity with insufficient control over their subsidiary to be held liable for the harm. In the latter two cases the judges decided the Court did not have jurisdiction to hear the claims while in *Lungowe v. Vedanta* the claimants were successful.

Vedanta has challenged the ruling and the case will be heard in the Supreme Court in January 2019. Nonetheless, the courts have on the face of it given contradictory and confusing guidance. Parliament must respond by reforming the law to clarify parent companies' responsibilities and liabilities for human rights abuses. Here are four reasons why:

1. Victims face insurmountable barriers to justice in their home country.

The current case against UK-headquartered mining company Vedanta and its Zambian subsidiary Konkola Copper Mines (KCM) was brought by 1,826 Zambian villagers, who contend that highly toxic discharge from KCM's Nchanga copper mine is contaminating their water, causing illness, damaging crops and affecting fishing.

It would be virtually impossible for the villagers to obtain justice in Zambia, one of the world's poorest countries. No legal aid is available and conditional fee arrangements are also illegal. As subsistence farmers, the victims do not have the means to pay for legal representation. Moreover, at present Zambia's legal infrastructure is insufficient to handle such an unwieldy case. Previous similar cases have collapsed. KCM has also established a reputation for using every available means to delay cases and increase costs. Most worryingly, the judge in Nyansulu v KCM suggested that KCM—the largest private employer in Zambia—had previously been 'shielded from criminal prosecution by political connections and financial influence'.

This final point gets to the root of the problem. Multinational companies often bring huge inward investment to extremely poor countries. While this has obvious potential benefits, it creates a significant power imbalance that irresponsible companies can easily abuse.

2. Information vital to proving the claim is under lock and key with the companies.

The Court of Appeal dismissed the claims against Shell and Unilever due to an absence of evidence demonstrating that the parent companies had operational control over their subsidiaries.

The proceedings were still at an early stage and there was no requirement for the companies to disclose documents about the relationships in the corporate group. Instead, it was up to the victims to show that the parent companies were in control of their subsidiaries' operations at the time the harm occurred. In both cases, the claimants' evidence that centralised standards were set by the parent companies was deemed insufficient.

This places an unrealistic evidentiary burden on claimants, in a situation where there is already a huge inequality in access to information. Legislation on parent company liability could redress this imbalance by reversing the burden of proof to place a requirement on the parent company to show what steps it had taken to manage human rights standards in its operations and prevent the harm from occurring.

3. The UK government and UK multinationals have signed up to international standards on responsible business conduct.

In 2011 the UK government announced its commitment to implement the UNGPs. Two years later, it published the world's first National Action Plan on business and human rights, which included the government's expectation that UK businesses respect human rights throughout their operations.

Unilever is one of the few multinational companies that has committed to implementing the UNGPs. Shell states that its human rights approach is informed by the UNGPs 'and applies to all of our employees and contractors'.

But Unilever is now attempting to hide behind its corporate structure to block access to remedy for workers on its tea plantation who suffered serious human rights abuses during post-election violence in 2007. In Okpabi v Shell, the Court of Appeal decided that 'the importance of multi-national parent companies conducting themselves consistently with international standards' was irrelevant to the matter at hand, and a 'doubtful foundation for the imposition of a duty of care'.

As Amnesty International has pointed out, it is contradictory for UK courts to dismiss as irrelevant international normative frameworks that governments and businesses themselves are using to, respectively, set up their expectations of businesses and inform their steps to prevent negative human rights impacts across their global operations.[1]

The introduction of a mandatory requirement for companies to conduct human rights due diligence in line with the UNGPs would remove any doubt about the corporate responsibility to respect human rights and the associated liability for failure to do so.

4. There is a clear trend towards embedding the corporate responsibility to protect human rights into law

The 2017 French *devoir de vigilance* law requires large companies to implement "vigilance plans" to identify and prevent risks of human rights abuses in their business operations and supply chains. If a harm occurs the company can be held liable for failing to implement an adequate plan.

In Switzerland campaigners have gathered public support for a constitutional amendment to introduce mandatory human rights due diligence based on the UNGPs, with a provision to make Swiss based firms liable for human rights abuses and environmental violations caused abroad by companies under their control.

Discussions and campaigns about mandatory human rights due diligence are also taking place in Norway, Sweden, Spain, Italy, Germany, Luxembourg and The Netherlands.

Properly formulated, a mandatory requirement in the UK would benefit business as well as victims, by providing much-needed clarification of companies' responsibilities. Parliament should pass legislation enshrining the developing international standards on business and human rights to shift the burden of proof for victims; create less focus on a need to prove 'control' thereby mitigating against risk of parent companies distancing themselves from subsidiaries; and enable victims of environmental and human rights abuse to access justice.

Endnotes

[1] https://www.amnesty.org/download/Documents/AFR4483212018ENGLISH.PD

Periodical and Internet Sources Bibliography

The following articles have been selected to supplement the diverse views presented in this chapter.

Aisha Dodwell, "Corporations Rule the World? Not Quite. But We Must Stop Them While We Still Can," *Ecologist*, 13 September 2016. https://theecologist.org/2016/sep/13/corporations-rule-world-not-quite-we-must-stop-them-while-we-still-can

Maria Hengeveld, "Big Business Has a New Scam: 'The Purpose Paradigm,'" *Nation*, January 4, 2019. https://www.thenation.com/article/big-business-has-a-new-scam-the-purpose-paradigm/

Parag Khanna, "The Rise of the Titans," *Foreign Policy*, March/April 2016.

Justin Kuepper, "The Impact of Globalization on Economic Growth," The Balance, updated November 19, 2018. https://www.thebalance.com/globalization-and-its-impact-on-economic-growth-1978843

Reihan Salam, "Who Needs Advisory Boards?" *National Review*, September 11, 2017. https://www.nationalreview.com/magazine/2017/09/11/donald-trump-advisory-boards-who-needs-them/

Matt Timms, "The Relationship between Corporations and Climate Change," *World Finance*, March 10, 2016. https://www.worldfinance.com/special-reports/the-relationship-between-corporations-and-climate-change

Bruce Upbin, "The 147 Companies that Control Everything," *Forbes*, October 22, 2011. https://www.forbes.com/sites/bruceupbin/2011/10/22/the-147-companies-that-control-everything/#24c7c2bf5105

World Bank Group, "How Developing Countries Can Get the Most out of Direct Investment," World Bank, October 25, 2017. https://www.worldbank.org/en/topic/competitiveness/publication/global-investment-competitiveness-report

GLOBALVIEWPOINTS

CHAPTER 3

Corporate Dominance and Democracy

VIEWPOINT 1

Who Runs the World?
David Smith

In previous chapters, various authors have mentioned how the dominance of global corporations affects democracy. In the following viewpoint David Smith examines the question "who runs the world" through a historical lens and finds a more nuanced answer than we've yet seen. After discussing the predictions of a political scientist in the 1970s, the author begins by giving statistics that show the extent and power of multinational corporations over the years and how governments have responded. David Smith is economics editor of the Sunday Times *and is author of several books on economics.*

As you read, consider the following questions:

1. What were political scientist Joseph Nye's predictions mentioned here about the future of large corporations? Did they come true?
2. Why does this author call investment banks "the modern masters of the universe"?
3. What, according to this viewpoint, did Nye mean by the phrase "soft power"?

It is more than 40 years since Joseph Nye, the American political scientist, wrote his seminal article on multinational corporations for *Foreign Affairs*, the journal on international politics produced by the US Council on Foreign Relations. Nye's

"Who Runs the World?" by David Smith, Originally commissioned from White Light Media by Equatex, September 21, 2015. Reprinted by Permission.

article, 'Multinationals: The Games and the Rules: Multinational Corporations in World Politics', was addressing what at the time was a growing phenomenon: large businesses operating across borders and increasingly exerting considerable power over governments.

As he put it: "As dramatic as the rise of the multinational corporation has been its increased political prominence." While attracting inward investment from these new leviathans of the world economy brought benefits, many governments even then had come to fear this kind of economic takeover as their predecessors had been concerned about military invasion.

And, predicted Nye in 1974: "The odds are that both the size and political impact of multinationals will continue to grow … Predictions that 300 giant corporations will run the world economy tend to be based on simple projections of past ten-percent annual growth rates, and fail to take into account some of the disadvantages that appear with large size, particularly in manufacturing, when temporary monopoly advantages have been competed away. The challenge to governments will come more from global scope and mobility than from corporate size. Even smaller multinationals can make crucial allocative decisions that challenge the welfare goals of governments. Corporate mobility (which is greater in service and some manufacturing than in extractive industries) is not only a challenge to small states, but also to large states like the United States."

Not "Coca-Colonization"

Nye was right about the continued rise of multinationals and that their power and influence would be exerted in a more subtle way than the "Coca-Colonization" feared in the 1970s. Global businesses have learned to become more culturally aware as they have become larger. Even so, most modern economic developments would not have occurred without the multinationals that were all-powerful back then, and the new ones that have emerged since. Globalisation is not the result of countries interacting with each other but corporations. They drive the trade and investment flows that provide the fuel for economic growth. Perhaps the most significant modern economic change—the rise of China as it emerged from behind its closed and protected walls – would not have happened without Western-based multinationals. They were the ones that invested in the People's Republic, used it as an export base, and opened it up to the world economy.

The rise of these global corporations has often appeared unstoppable. It is hard, for example, to think of the American economy without the contribution of US-based multinationals. A McKinsey Global Institute study, published on the eve of the global financial crisis, found that while US multinationals accounted for fewer than 1% of all American businesses in 2007, they generated 23% of private sector gross domestic product (measured by value-added). Even more impressively, they had contributed 31% of the gains in real GDP and 41% of the gains in productivity since 1990.

"While their activities create 23% of US private sector value added, they account for larger shares of productivity growth and US private R&D spending," McKinsey said. "They pay higher average wages than other US companies. They account for almost half of the nation's exports and more than a third of its imports, resulting in a more favorable trade balance than other US companies. US multinationals also exert a significant indirect, or 'multiplier,' effect on the economy, which magnifies their contributions further."

American Dominance Persists

Despite the rise of China and of mega firms from Europe, Japan and other Far Eastern countries, US-based multinationals still dominate. The annual Fortune Global 500 list is a ranking of these big beasts in the world's corporate jungle, who between them account for $31.2 trillion of revenues and $1.7 trillion in profits. The two figures are not directly comparable, but as an illustration, the $31 trillion of global 500 revenues compares with global GDP of around $75 trillion. It is the equivalent, in other words, of more than 40% of the world's GDP. These 500 companies employ more than 65 million people between them.

Though there are firms from 36 countries that rank large enough to feature in the Fortune Global 500, America still dominates with 128, more than a quarter, followed by China with 95, Japan with 57, France with 31, Britain and Germany with 28 each, South Korea with 17, Switzerland and the Netherlands with 13 each and Canada with 10. America's Walmart, the world's biggest corporation, was instrumental in locating production in China and has operations globally. Many of the other global giants, including China's Sinopec, BP, Royal Dutch Shell and ExxonMobil, are in the oil industry.

Not all the world's biggest companies would meet the definition of a true global corporation, particularly in China, where for some firms size mainly reflects domestic turnover. Most, however, do. Again, comparisons between GDP and corporate revenues are imperfect, but they show that Walmart would have ranked as the 28th largest economy in the world in 2013, with Royal Dutch Shell as 29th, ExxonMobil as 30th and Sinopec as 31st, all of them with bigger revenues than the GDPs of, for example, Austria, South Africa, Thailand, Denmark, Singapore and Nigeria. A top 100 of global economies and global corporations would include 37 international businesses among its numbers.

Does that mean that multinationals, not governments, run the world? Combine even a few of these like-minded businesses and you are talking, if not of world government by big corporations, but of an enormous concentration of potential power. When politicians rub shoulders with CEOs at the Davos World Economic Forum in the Swiss Alps each January, the question of which of them genuinely has their hands on the levers of power is a valid one.

When Nye posed the question more than 40 years ago, he thought that the answer was no, and would remain so. Multinationals would interact with governments, and often there would be a lot of tension in that interaction, but extrapolating the rise of the global corporation and ending with world domination was probably not going to happen.

A few years ago, you could have been forgiven for thinking that this was too cautious a prediction. If the global corporation of the

1970s was most likely to be found in manufacturing, the big players by the eve of the financial crisis—in power and influence if not in turnover—were in the financial services sector. Investment banks, the modern masters of the universe, appeared to run the world economy. Goldman Sachs helped the Greek government make its public finances look more respectable and invented the concept of the BRICs (Brazil, Russia, India and China). The investment banking community called the shots. In America, pressure from the industry led to the scrapping of most of the Glass-Steagall Act, the legislation adopted in the 1930s to restrain risky banking activity.

Even Labour's Gordon Brown, who had been suspicious of the banking community in his early days as Chancellor of the Exchequer, was won over. In his final Mansion House speech in June 2007 before becoming prime minister, he was fulsome in his praise. "The financial services sector in Britain, and the City of London at the centre of it, is a great example of a highly skilled, high value added, talent driven industry that shows how we can excel in a world of global competition," he said. "Britain needs more of the vigour, ingenuity and aspiration that you demonstrate that is the hallmark of your success."

His timing was unfortunate, and the financial crisis that quickly followed changed the nature of the relationship between governments and big business. The big banks, having called the shots for a quarter of a century, now needed to be rescued by those governments. Royal Bank of Scotland, the biggest bank in the world on the eve of the crisis, had to be rescued by the British government, while protesting that it remained solvent. Its acerbic chief executive, Fred Goodwin, was stripped of his knighthood. Most of Wall Street needed a bailout, following the collapse of one of its number, Lehman Brothers.

When Joseph Nye was writing about multinationals in the 1970s, America's car companies were prominent among them. In the financial crisis they needed emergency help from the American government to keep going. Chrysler, Ford and General Motors lobbied for aid to see them through the crisis and eventually got it, though this did not prevent GM, seen as the bellwether of the US economy ("what's good for General Motors is good for America") from temporary bankruptcy. How much did these rescues, often humiliating for these big businesses and the people who ran them, change the dynamic? Was it just a short break in the rise of global corporate power, or something more fundamental?

Some see the impact of the 2007–09 crisis as long lasting, implying a decisive shift in the balance of power between corporations and governments. Though economies have shown themselves to be vulnerable, and in the case of countries such as Greece that vulnerability persists, economies survive. Corporations, in contrast, and most notably the banks, would not have survived without government and central bank support. Some see a new post-crisis form of capitalism, in which collaboration rather than confrontation between business and government becomes the norm. Others, such Mariana Mazzucato, professor in the economics of innovation at Sussex University, argue that this has always been the case.

In her new book *The Entrepreneurial State*, she argues that the public sector has often been the driving force behind what are generally regarded as private sector innovations, including in information technology. As she puts it, the book "challenges the image of the lethargic, regulating state versus the dynamic business sector—using historical examples to show how some of the most high risk and courageous investments that led to revolutions in IT biotechnology and nanotechnology, were sparked by public sector institutions. It offers a new way of thinking about political economy in the 21st century."

The Governments' Response? Regulation

Whether or not this is a generally accepted view, governments have been sharpening their claws in their dealings with big business in the post-crisis era. This has been most obvious in the case of the banks, which have been subject to tougher regulation, higher capital requirements and special taxes such as Britain's bank levy. There has also been additional pressure to ensure that multinationals do not try to minimise their tax bills. The technology giants, in particular, have been widely criticised and have come under pressure to pay their fair share of tax.

The Australian government recently announced a multinational anti-avoidance law, which will take effect at the start of 2016. Companies dealing with Australian customers will be expected to pay an appropriate amount of Australian tax. As the Australian Treasury puts it: "Approximately 30 large multinational companies are suspected of diverting profits using artificial structures to avoid a taxable presence in Australia. Where the law applies, multinationals will be subject to the Government's new doubled penalty regime for tax avoidance and profit shifting schemes. This means that not only will tax avoiders need to pay the tax that they owe, they will also face penalties of up to 100% of the tax they owe and interest."

So the relationship between big business and governments is constantly evolving. There are times when the balance shifts sharply in favour of corporations, and times when it shifts back. The latest book from Nye, to return to where we started, is called *Is the American Century Over?* He concluded that it is not, despite all the emphasis in recent years on the rise of China. Soft power, the concept popularised by Nye, includes the global influence of a country's businesses and the worldwide importance of a country's brands. In both respects, America is in a strong position. There may be friction between businesses and governments. Mostly, however, they are pulling in the same direction.

VIEWPOINT 2

In the United States Corporate Capture Threatens Democratic Government

Liz Kennedy

In the following viewpoint, Liz Kennedy gets into the details of how corporations influence government both from without by making political donations and lobbying, and from within when corporate leaders and lobbyists accept positions in the governments of candidates they supported. She argues that citizens have a moral obligation to future generations to protect the system of self-government from the greed of big business. Liz Kennedy is a senior fellow of the Center for American Progress.

As you read, consider the following questions:

1. What is the "revolving door" described in this viewpoint?
2. Here the author points out that corporate influence on the US government goes back to the nation's founding. What does she note has changed?
3. In what ways beyond donations to candidates do corporations wield influence over the government?

America faces a crisis of corporate capture of democratic government, where the economic power of corporations has been translated into political power with disastrous effects for

"Corporate Capture Threatens Democratic Government," by Liz Kennedy, Center for American Progress, March 29, 2017. Reprinted by permission.

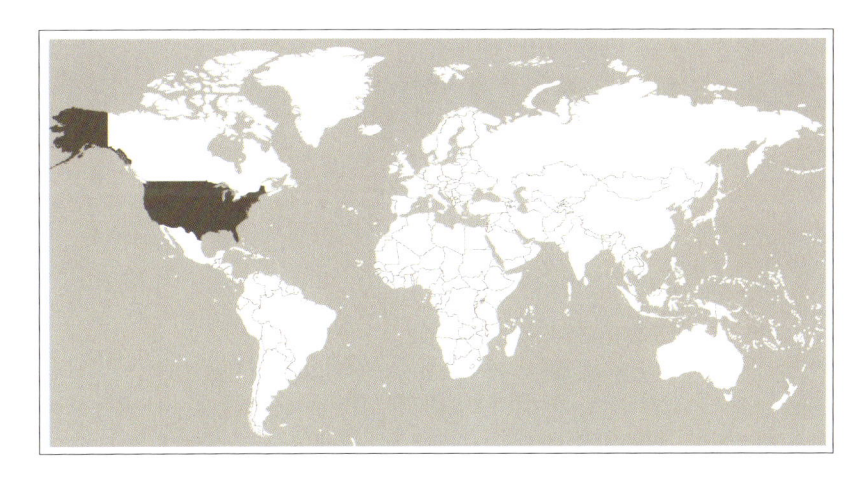

people's lives. In his new book, *Captured: The Corporate Infiltration of American Democracy*, Sen. Sheldon Whitehouse (D-RI) warns that "corporations of vast wealth and remorseless staying power have moved into our politics to seize for themselves advantages that can be seized only by control over government." The book illustrates what he calls, the "immense pressure deployed by the corporate sector in our government." We must rebalance our democracy by changing the rules to limit the power of money over government and empower people to engage politically as a countervailing force.

Currently, the domination of big money over our public institutions prevents government from being responsive to Americans. This certainly is not a new phenomenon—but it is growing. Even in 2009, before the *Citizens United v. FEC* ruling removed constraints on corporate political spending, 80 percent of Americans agreed with the following statement:

> I am worried that large political contributions will prevent Congress from tackling the important issues facing American today, like the economic crisis, rising energy costs, reforming health care, and global warming.

In the first presidential contest after the *Citizens United* decision, 84 percent of Americans agreed that corporate political spending drowns out the voices of average Americans, and 83 percent believed that corporations and corporate CEOs have too much political power and influence. This aligns with more recent research showing that 84 percent of people think government is benefitting special interests, and 83 percent think government is benefitting big corporations and the wealthy.

As already noted, the undue influence of corporate interests on the functions of government is not new, and Sen. Whitehouse's book explains how Americans have faced and overcome this threat before. America's founders recognized the danger of corporate capture: In 1816, Thomas Jefferson warned the new republic to "crush in its birth the aristocracy of our monied corporations which dare already to challenge our government to a trial of strength, and bid defiance to the laws of their country." Almost a century later, President Theodore Roosevelt, in his annual address to Congress in 1907, said:

> The fortunes amassed through corporate organization are now so large, and vest such power in those that wield them, as to make it a matter of necessity to give to the sovereign—that is, to the Government, which represents the people as a whole— some effective power of supervision over their corporate use.

President Roosevelt was responsible for the first federal ban on corporate political contributions. But now America's rules for using money in politics are out of date, and our system of government is out of balance. The Supreme Court's conservative majority has turned its back on reasonable limits for how concentrated wealth can be used to shape government and public choices. In 2010, *Citizens United* allowed corporate money to be used to support or attack candidates and influence American elections. Previously, in a case overruled by *Citizens United*, the Court upheld corporate political spending rules, decrying "the corrosive and distorting effects of immense aggregations of wealth that are accumulated with the help of the corporate form and that have little or no correlation to the public's support for the corporation's political ideas." In his book, Sen. Whitehouse calls out the Supreme Court's conservative majority, which has "obediently repaid the corporate powers by changing the basic operating systems of our democracy in ways that consistently give big corporate powers even more power in our process of government, rewiring our democracy to corporate advantage."

Corporate interests can vastly outspend labor or public interest groups on elections. For example, in 2014, business interests spent $1.1 billion on state candidates and committees compared to the $215 million that labor groups spent. That same year, business political action committees, or PACs, spent nearly $380 million in federal elections, while labor union PACs gave close to $60 million. In 2016, it is estimated that $1 out of every $8 that went to super PACs came from corporate sources. Super PACs—which didn't exist before 2010—raised almost $1.8 billion for the 2016 elections. Recently developed dark money channels have exploded, and more than $800 million dollars of political spending with no disclosure of donors has occurred since 2010. This denies voters information and blocks accountability by hiding the identity of political spenders who want to push their agendas and points of view without leaving fingerprints. Dark money has led to an increase in negative campaigning and deceptive statements in political advertisements, feeding the politics of destruction.

Moreover, the anti-democratic influence of money in politics doesn't end on election day. The dominance of corporations and business interests exists not just in election spending but also in lobbying elected officials and decision-makers. In 2012, an important study of political influence, *Unheavenly Chorus,* looked at organized-interest activity aimed at influencing policymaking in Washington, D.C.. According to the study, social welfare and labor organization made up just 2 percent of all organized-interest activity—corporations, trade associations, and business groups accounted for 48 percent. Corporations and business groups spend much more on lobbying than organizations that represent large constituencies of Americans. For example, between 1998 and 2016, OpenSecrets.org reports that the U.S. Chamber of Commerce—just one of many groups advocating for the interests of big business—

spent $1.3 billion on lobbying the federal government compared to $720 million spent by all labor unions.

Corporate influence over government does not end with the passing of a law. Corporate entities with no natural limits and endless resources can wage a long-term, sustained attack across policymaking pressure points. For example, if a law is passed that corporate interests oppose, relentless industry pressure can be brought to bear on the agencies charged with enforcing that legislation. Again, in his book, Sen. Whitehouse describes "heavy lawyering of the rulemaking and enforcement processes, often as simple brute pressure to cause delay and cost" on the part of corporate interests. Furthermore, any final rule may be challenged in courts that are increasingly friendly to corporate forces at the expense of people.

In the short time that President Donald Trump has been in office, the revolving door between industry and the federal agencies regulating them is back in full swing thanks to the administration loosening restrictions on lobbyists taking posts at agencies they previously sought to influence on behalf corporate clients. The independent nonprofit newsroom ProPublica discovered dozens of federally registered lobbyists who were among the first Trump appointees to take positions in federal agencies. For example, lobbyists for the pharmaceutical industry and health insurance companies are now in key posts at the U.S. Department of Health and Human Services; a lobbyist for the construction industry who fought wage and worker safety standards now works for the U.S. Department of Labor; a lobbyist for the extractive resources industry is now at the U.S. Department of Energy; and a for-profit college lobbyist who sought to weaken protections for students worked at the U.S. Department of Education.

In the Trump administration, as noted by Eric Lipton at *The New York Times*, we continue to see "the merging of private business interest with government affairs." In just one example, billionaire investor Carl Icahn has been named "special adviser to the president," but because he is not officially a government employee, he is not subject to the same conflict of interest divestment requirements. As a consequence, Icahn maintains his majority holdings in an oil refinery while zealously advocating for a rule change that would have saved his refinery more than $200 million the previous year. We have reached an apotheosis of concentrated wealth running government for their interests—Trump's cabinet has more wealth than one-third of American households, and Icahn is wealthier than all of them combined.

Captured: The Corporate Infiltration of American Democracy tells hard truths about the central threat posed by the rule of the rich—plutocracy—and how it is overwhelming American democracy. Sen. Whitehouse writes, "Corporate money is calling the tune in Congress; Congress is unwilling or unable to stand up to corporate power (indeed, Congress is often its agent)." These are truths that must be faced to be fixed.

Our democratic society must demonstrate its resilience and return to core American principles and values of government that serve the people. We have the power to demand that Congress break the nexus between Wall Street and Washington that keeps the rules of our economy rigged to benefit the wealthiest few at the expense of the many. Americans can resist the slide to secret political spending and require disclosure for the big money interests behind our toxic politics of personal destruction. We can demand that lobbyists be prohibited from acting as fundraisers. And, amidst the shocking scandal of Russian interference in America's democracy, we can insist that Congress ban foreign corporate money in elections.

Let us harbor no illusions—this battle won't be easy, but that doesn't mean it is impossible. Ever since our founding as a republic, Americans have fought to expand democratic freedoms and protect democratic society from being corrupted through unchecked private greed and undermined through grotesque inequality. One can clearly see the result of corporate power over policy in the present levels of wealth inequality—unmatched since the Great Depression—where all the economic gains in the past several years accrued to the wealthiest 1 percent. But as Economist Thomas Piketty concluded his study of economic inequality in *Capital in the Twenty-First Century* by writing, "If we are to regain control of capitalism, we must bet everything on democracy."

For democracy to work, the rules must be rewritten to prevent corporate capture of government and to create a system that supports fair representation for all Americans. Whether we fight to preserve our free system of self-government for ourselves and posterity is not a choice—it is a moral obligation.

Viewpoint 3

Citizens Must Work to Contain and Shape Corporate Power

K. Sabeel Rahman

In the following viewpoint K. Sabeel Rahman discusses two books on the subject of how corporate power subverts democracy, one that gives a history of court decisions that led to the power corporations now hold in the United States and one that presents a variety of essays on the subject from different scholars. Together the books make clear, says Rahman, that reformers have always been key in containing corporate power and making sure the people have a voice. K. Sabeel Rahman is an associate professor of law at Brooklyn Law School.

As you read, consider the following questions:

1. How, according to the scholars discussed in this viewpoint, have both conservatives and liberals used corporate rights for social purposes?
2. How does this author explain the "dual nature" of corporations?
3. How, according to this author, have citizens responded over the years to changes in corporate power over democracy?

With the passage of a massive corporate tax cut, a billionaire's cabinet in Washington, and rising corporate profits amidst worsening economic inequality and insecurity, the problem of

---

Used with the permission of The American Prospect, "Corporate Power and the Unmaking of American Democracy," by K. Sabeel Rahman. ©The American Prospect, Prospect.org, 2018. All rights reserved.

corporate power is justifiably at the forefront of political debate. A pair of new books provide a rich historical context for understanding these tensions between corporate power, democracy, and inequality: legal scholar Adam Winkler's *We the Corporations,* and a volume edited by historians Naomi Lamoreaux and William Novak called *Corporations and American Democracy.* Taken together, these volumes show how corporations have historically leveraged law and public policy to secure far greater rights and influence.

Winkler, a constitutional law scholar at UCLA Law School, offers a comprehensive account of how corporate legal rights emerged, from the colonial era to *Citizens United* and the contemporary battles over corporate speech and campaign spending. Winkler's account makes clear that corporate powers have always been a legal construction. The question is not whether corporations should have "more" or "less" power; rather it is about what rights and powers corporations should have, for what purposes.

In the colonial era, corporate entities like the Massachusetts Bay Company were central to facilitating collective action, association, and economic activity. Winkler's book then narrates key historical turning points where a combination of corporate actors, lawyers, and judges made crucial decisions establishing corporate rights, and transforming the nature of both the corporation and the American polity itself. The first key turning point came in the 1809 case of *Bank of the United States v. Deveaux*, in which Chief Justice John Marshall held that corporations were to be understood as associations of persons. In this view, corporate rights were limited, and ultimately derivative of the rights of their (human) members. It wasn't until 1886 in the famous case of *Santa Clara County v. Southern Pacific Railroad* that the Supreme Court established the legal fiction of corporate personhood itself.

But as Winkler argues, these advances in corporate rights, perhaps paradoxically, served more than the narrow interests of corporate litigants. Corporations and the lawyers representing them, in Winkler's account, have been at the vanguard of legal innovation and transformation, often forging property and liberty rights that have sometimes advanced as well as narrowed American democracy. Both the associative and personhood views of the corporation served as grounding for subsequent cases finding specific property rights and protections against government pressure, and later liberty rights including speech rights for corporations.

Crucially, these rights emerged from "liberal" and "conservative" courts alike, and often served a variety of social purposes. Corporate property interests were key to the emergence of early Fourth and Fifth Amendment criminal procedure protections against search and seizure and on due process grounds. Similarly, speech rights were key to protecting media companies from threats of censorship and attack by state actors—including demagogues like Huey Long. The NAACP leveraged corporate association arguments to protect its membership from state-sanctioned harassment and pressure as Southern governments sought to criminalize the civil rights movement activists.

Winkler's account is thus partly a powerful theory of legal change and societal transformation. Through strategic litigation motivated by corporate self-interest, corporations—and their representatives in the legal profession—worked massive transformations in American law, public policy, and democracy itself. As Winkler argues, corporations have been adept at harnessing the top legal talent—from the days of Daniel Webster to the present—and pursuing risky, innovative legal claims. Corporations are thus, for Winkler, "constitutional leveragers" and "constitutional first movers."

Winkler is admirably balanced in his account, adding nuance to the conventional right/left debates by avoiding simple pro- or anti-corporate power narratives. But even as these corporate rights often have afterlives that cut in a variety of directions, on net the story of corporate-driven legal innovation is not a neutral one. It is not a coincidence that corporate rights gained traction in our legal jurisprudence well before equal rights for African Americans or women—Winkler notes that the 1809 corporate rights cases predate by decades cases like *Dred Scott v. Sandford* (1857) and *Bradwell v. Illinois* (1873), which considered and ultimately ruled against legal rights for enslaved persons and women, respectively.

After the passage of the 14th Amendment, aimed at overturning Dred Scott and ensuring birthright citizenship, more than 300 of the roughly 600 cases brought under the amendment from 1868 to 1912 addressed the rights of corporations; only 28 were about the rights of African American persons. Furthermore, corporate rights were implicated in decisions that reaffirmed racial and economic inequalities—like *Plessy v. Ferguson* maintaining segregation—and Lochner-era cases striking down labor and economic regulations advanced by the emerging labor movement in the face of the inequities of industrialization. As Winkler suggests, the result was to transform the 14th Amendment into what one observer at the time called "the Magna Charta of accumulated and organized capital."

Even more galling are the episodes recounted by Winkler in which corporate interests and their allies in the legal profession and the judiciary constructed these favorable regimes using legal sleights of hand. Winkler uncovers how the *Santa Clara* decision, cited by hundreds of cases as precedent for assuring corporate personhood and the legal rights that follow, in fact held no such thing. Rather, through the combined efforts of railroad magnate Leland Stanford, his legal team, and a favorably inclined Supreme Court Justice Stephen Field, the case was improperly summarized in a Court report—and then cited for this holding that Field (and Stanford) supported but had been unable to actually secure in the original case itself.

In the modern era, the turning point came in the 1970s, when Supreme Court Justice Lewis Powell, himself a former lobbyist with the U.S. Chamber of Commerce and architect of the chamber's deliberate strategy of dismantling New Deal economic regulations through a litigation strategy aimed at the courts, was able to put his views into practice in a series of decisions that formed the foundations for modern corporate speech doctrine—and ultimately

Citizens United. Indeed, Winkler's book is in part an important reminder that the levers for corporate influence extend far beyond the familiar realm of campaign financing and lobbying; if anything, the most valuable vector for the construction of corporate power has been their skilled leveraging of law, litigation, and the judiciary itself. Corporate rights may have been central to forging many of our vital legal precedents, but we the people have still been junior partners at best in this trajectory, in a legal history that has largely been driven by and for those corporate interests.

In *Corporations and American Democracy*, historians Naomi Lamoreaux, William Novak, and their colleagues offer an equally sweeping and compelling account of these tensions between corporate power, law, inequality, and democracy. The volume includes a number of important contributions in the legal history of corporate rights and corporate personhood, including essays by Margaret Blair, Elizabeth Pollman, Ruth Bloch, Naomi Lamoreaux, and Winkler himself. These essays as a whole deepen some of the themes from Winkler's book: that corporate rights have been products of legal contestation; that those rights have at times been secured through theories of corporations-as-association as well as theories of corporations-as-persons. Indeed, the modern view of corporate personhood with thick legal rights is, as these essays suggest, built on a dual misapprehension. On the one hand, there is a danger to having a monolithic view of corporate legal rights when the history of the corporation reveals a stunning multiplicity of corporate forms and purposes, each warranting wildly different kinds of protections and limits. On the other hand, the modern legal regime around corporate rights, including Citizens United, significantly underplays the very real concentrations of economic and political power that these corporations exercise, often without regard to the interests of all of their supposed (human) members.

As the editors argue, the tensions around corporate power also stem from the dual nature of corporations themselves: "On the one hand, the corporation has long been seen as a useful and alluring vehicle for harnessing and distributing the collective

The Dominance of Global Corporations

> ### Facebook Admits Failings over Incitement to Violence in Myanmar
>
> In April, the Guardian reported that hate speech on Facebook in Myanmar had exploded during the Rohingya crisis, which was caused by a crackdown by the military in Rahkine state in August 2017. Tens of thousands of Rohingya were killed, raped and assaulted, villages were razed to the ground and more than 700,000 Rohingya fled over the border to Bangladesh.
>
> The recent UN fact-finding mission to Myanmar, which concluded a genocide had taken place against the Rohingya in Rahkine, specifically singled out the role of Facebook in fanning the flames of anti-Muslim sentiment and violence.
>
> Alex Warofka, a Facebook product policy manager, said in a blog post that the report demonstrated that "prior to this year, we weren't doing enough to help prevent our platform from being used to foment division and incite offline violence. We agree that we can and should do more."
>
> The company said they were tackling the problem, this year hiring 100 native Myanmar speakers to review content. The company took action on around 64,000 pieces of content in Myanmar for violating hate speech policies in 2018. They also took down 18 accounts and 52 pages associated with figures in the Myanmar military who were named in

energies of individuals—an engine of economic growth." Yet at the same time, corporations have also been "viewed with suspicion as a potentially dangerous threat … a site of coercion, monopoly, and the agglomeration of excessive social, economic, and political power." Where Winkler's book tells the story of modern legal rights being constructed in large part through corporate-driven litigation, the *Corporations* volume tells a similar story on a much broader canvas: These essays suggest that the very institutions of American democracy themselves are products of battles over corporate power—both the efforts to defend them, and the efforts to rein them in.

Thus, essays like those by Eric Hilt, Jessica Hennessey, and John Wallis suggest that early legal battles establishing general incorporation laws were more than a power grab by corporate

> the UN fact-finding report as being involved in the genocide and ethnic cleansing in Rahkine.
>
> However, the BSR report made it clear that due to the "complex social and political context of Myanmar" the social media giant did not yet have the problem under control and there was still a "high likelihood" of hate speech being posted on Facebook in Myanmar.
>
> The report said the consequences for the victims of this hate speech on Facebook, they said, was "severe, with lives and bodily integrity placed at risk from incitement to violence."
>
> One interviewee quoted in the report said: "Activists are being harassed, self-censorship exists, and activity on Facebook today is closing freedom of expression, rather than increasing it. One side is shutting down the other, and it is no longer a marketplace of ideas."
>
> In particular, the report highlighted the upcoming 2020 general elections in Myanmar as a cause for concern.
>
> "Today's challenging circumstances are likely to escalate in the run-up to the election, and Facebook would be well-served by preparing for multiple eventualities now," the reports authors warned.
>
> *"Facebook Admits Failings over Incitement to Violence in Myanmar," by Hannah Ellis-Petersen, Guardian News and Media Limited, November 6, 2018.*

entities. Rather, this shift was crucial for reining in rampant corruption in the patronage-based granting of special charters by state officials. Corporate rights, in this domain, were vital to creating a foundation for economic dynamism and genuine political liberty. But this was not always the case. Essays like those by Daniel Crane, Ajay Mehrotra, Novak, and Steven Bank shift to the industrial era of the late 19th and early 20th century, and together paint a different picture. Here, as corporate power magnified in the era of trusts, monopolies, and the specter of industrialized production, the challenge was not how to protect corporations and people from a corrupt state, but rather how to use the state to protect people against arbitrary and exploitative corporations. Thus, efforts by reformers to impose legal limits on corporate power led to the emergence of modern democratic institutions, from the tax regime to the regulatory state—public-sector instrumentalities that did not exist previously. These institutions, so central to modern democratic governance, emerged out of the urgent struggle by reformers to create new institutions and laws that could provide a countervailing balance against corporate behemoths, from the trusts to the industrialized workplace.

The volume concludes by suggesting that this struggle over protecting the socially valuable activities of corporations while limiting the dangerous excesses of corporate power will continue, sometimes in new forms. Nelson Lichtenstein's essay notes that the shift from large vertically integrated firms to more diffuse supply chains has been central to the erosion of the safety net and the increasingly precarious forms of modern work, undermining those turn-of-the-century protections for workers and consumers even as corporations are able to centralize greater power through strategic use of outsourcing, franchising, and platforms. Winkler's own contribution to the volume returns to the *Citizens United* decision as an example of how a 19th-century vision of corporations-as-association has helped sanction dangerous new forms of 21st-century corporate power in the political arena.

Indeed, while both books are framed as historical accounts of the rise of corporate power, these volumes can also be read as telling a vital parallel narrative: not of "we the corporations" but of "we the people" developing new movements, laws, rights, and institutions to contain corporate power, and channel it productively. Winkler touches on the importance of figures like Louis Brandeis, Thurgood Marshall, Ruth Bader Ginsburg, and Ralph Nader, to name a few—all lawyers who saw a valuable role for corporations and leveraged corporate rights strategically to serve larger visions of equality and democracy. But they also worked to establish vital guardrails, ways of limiting corporate power to prevent overreach. Similarly, the essays in the *Corporations* volume paint a similar picture, as the rise of antitrust law, public utility regulation, labor rights, and general forms of state taxation and regulation in the late 19th century were crucial in reining in the excesses of the first Gilded Age, and setting up the potential for a more egalitarian economy in the decades to come. As we struggle with new forms of corporate power, radical transformations to the nature of work, and growing inequities in our politics, these volumes offer invaluable reminders: that corporations ultimately are instruments whose powers and limits can serve a variety of economic, social, and political purposes; that corporations have been adept at shaping law and institutions—and that the prospect for a more inclusive economy and polity have always depended on the ability of reformers to mobilize and assert their own vision of appropriately contained corporate power.

Viewpoint 4

The Rise of Corporate Power Was the Fall of Democracy

Richard Moser

In the following viewpoint Richard Moser begins by putting democracy in the past tense. He argues that democracy was finally killed in the 1970s after a fusion of corporations with the state. The author outlines the reasons corporate power is incompatible with democracy, then calls for an overthrow of what he calls the "corporate dictatorship." Richard Moser is an activist and writer.

As you read, consider the following questions:

1. Why does this author call corporations such as Facebook, Google, and Twitter "so-called private corporations"?
2. When, according to this viewpoint, did corporations make "their first big power grab"?
3. What does they author say is corporate power's one reason for existing?

The rise of Corporate Power was the fall of democracy. Over the long haul, US politics has revolved around a deep tension between democracy and an unrelenting drive for plunder, power and empire. Granted that our democracy has been seriously flawed and only rarely revolutionary, yet the democratic movements are the source of every good thing America has ever stood for.

"How Corporate Power Killed Democracy," by Richard Moser, Counter Punch, December 6, 2017. Reprinted by permission.

Since the mid-1970s, when the corporations fused with the state, a new imperial order emerged that killed what remained of representative democracy. Not only would corporations exercise public authority as only government once had, but government would coordinate and serve corporate activity. Power and profits became one and the same. Corporate power has replaced democracy with oligarchy and justice with a vast militarized penal system. Instead of innovative production, they plunder people and planet.

To achieve this new order, elections and the economy had to be drained of any remaining democratic content. Both Democrats and Republicans were eager to have at it.

By the 1990s "Third Way" Democrats like Bill Clinton abandoned what was left of the New Deal to try to outdo the Republicans as the party of Wall Street. The Republicans pioneered election fraud on a national scale in 2000, 2004, and 2016; a lesson the Democrats learned all too well by the 2016 Primary. Neither major party wants election reform since free and fair elections would threaten the system itself.

So-called private corporations like Facebook, Google and Twitter control information and manage the 1st Amendment. The corporate media now broadcast propaganda and play the role of censor once monopolized by the FBI and CIA. The migration of propaganda work to civilian organizations began under Ronald Reagan.

While both major parties offer the people nothing beyond austerity and the worst kind of identity politics, the big banks like Goldman Sachs gained positions of real influence with both Republican and Democratic administrations and always with the Department of the Treasury and the Federal Reserve. Without pubic money and political protection the banking system—the headquarters of the mythical free market—could not function.

The Rise of Corporate Power

Corporations made the first big power grab in 1913 when the Federal Reserve was created. Banks were given the power to impose corporate regulation on the "cutthroat competition" of the free market. Competition was chaotic and lowered profits. Corporations killed not just democracy but the free market as well.

Corporations also had their own private militarized police force. The Pinkertons, infamous for attacking striking workers, was the largest armed force in the US in the early decades of the 20th century: larger than the US Army at that time.

The mid-1970s were nonetheless a pivotal time as corporations achieved unmatched political supremacy and overthrew a brief period of relative economic democracy. Corporate power was the reaction to the American revolution that occurred between 1955 and 1975.

The corporations wanted to lower wages while maintaining high levels of consumption and profit. Their solution was to deny workers raises while offering instead record levels of credit and debt. And for that move they needed massive banks. Finance capital then leveraged even greater profits by repackaging debt as an investment and selling the world on their scheme. And for that maneuver to work banks needed to act with the full faith and confidence of the US government.

The shift to austerity for workers and power for bankers began during the mid-1970's as wage increases no longer tracked productivity. During the last two years of the Carter Administration—with a majority Democratic congress—those trends continued and were dramatically accelerated by Reagan who empowered bankers, revised tax codes and redistributed wealth. By the 1990's the corporatization of government was more or less complete. Take Robert Rubin's career for example: he was a 26 year veteran of Goldman-Sachs and Bill Clinton's Treasury Secretary. Along with Henry Paulson, Alan Greenspan and Larry Summers, Rubin rewrote economic rules in the image of the corporation: a law unto themselves and in direct command of the power of the state.[1]

A well-funded revolving door insures the power of "Government-Sachs."

After the 2008 crash $19 trillion was destroyed as everyday people lost their homes, jobs and pensions but the banks received the largest global bailout in history. Big banks grew larger and more powerful than ever. Not only were there no indictments, but Obama returned Summers, Timothy Geithner and Ben Bernanke to power despite their roles as architects of the crisis. Hillary Clinton pandered to them, Trump railed against them, but after the 2016 election Trump appointed Goldman-Sachs executives to key postions.

Property is the Creature of the State

In order to kill the economic underpinnings of democracy, Corporate Power rigged the game. So deep is the fusion between the corporations and the state that profits are now created largely by political means. There is nothing "free" about this market; instead it is driven by political intervention every step of the way. From start to finish, the supply chain of corporate profits is government action.

- Big corporations, like Google, Facebook, and Apple start by appropriating technologies developed at the public expense by governments and universities.
- Corporations win billions in subsidies, including five $trillion a year for fossil fuels. Corporate power depends on what now seems a permanent regime of "quantitative easing" or virtually free money for finance capital.
- Workers are exploited for profit. Low wages and labor standards at home and abroad are enforced by law and trade agreements.
- Most discretionary spending in the US federal budget is for the military-industrial complex which is, with the possible exception of China, the largest centrally planned economy in the world.
- Tax codes permit and encourage corporations to avoid taxes and hoard capital. The amount staggers the imagination:

corporations and billionaires shelter between 21 and 31 $trillion from fair taxation, a sum equal to the GDP of the US and Japan combined. Political representatives enforce the fiction that the government is broke and austerity measures must be imposed.

- The corporate system still relies on plundering the natural world. The largest cost of resource extraction is environmental destruction. Pollution costs to the tune of 2.2 $trillion are "externalized" and taken off the corporate ledger books.

- Risk is externalized and the public pay. The government committed 16 $trillion to the bank bailout between 2008 and 2015.

If the true costs of risk, labor, research and development, environmental damage, war, and taxes were charged to their accounts, what corporation could claim profits? On environment costs alone, almost no industry would be profitable.

The fusion of the corporation and the state, not free-market capitalism, is the true political economy of the U.S.

The State is the Creature of Property

Want to kill democracy? Rig the elections and restrict political rights.

While there are many, many, many ways to prove that big money rules America, Supreme Court decision "Citizens United" provides compelling evidence that corporations wield state power. Instead of insuring that the people have protections like the Bill of Rights against the corporations that now govern, "Citizens United" repealed the 1st Amendment by recognizing corporations as people and protecting money as a form of free speech. Corporate power is cloaked and protected, the peoples' rights are stripped and rejected.

Justice Steven's dissenting opinion in "Citizens United" argued:

> The Court's…approach to the First Amendment may well promote corporate power at the cost of the individual and collective self-expression the Amendment was meant to serve. It will undoubtedly cripple the ability of ordinary citizens,

Congress, and the States to adopt even limited measures to protect against corporate domination of the electoral process."

The "corporate domination of the election process." Done.

Given that the top 0.1% is now worth as much as the bottom 90% and that long-standing inequalities in wealth have only increased during the Obama Administration and are sure to continue under Trump, the super-rich have the capacity to drown out all others voices and secure their domination of politics in the US.

The price tag for federal elections held in 2016 was $6.5 billion. A tidy sum for an election so bankrupt and dismal that over 90 million eligible voters stayed home and at least 1.75 million that did vote refused to do so for President. Millions more could do no better than hold their noses and vote, once again, for some fabled lesser of two evils.

Corporate Power Must Be Confronted

It's late in the day. In a 2014 study—the most comprehensive of its kind—Princeton and Northwestern University researchers have demonstrated the utter lack of democracy in the US. Corporate Power and the US Empire killed American democracy while political cowardice and propaganda have us looking for other perpetrators. No it's not the Russians. Its our own history, culture and political system.

Corporate power has created a world so unequal that there is no way to change it within the existing political framework. Teams of researchers using data that span thousands of years have concluded that the current extremes in wealth are setting the stage for conflict. In The Great Leveler, historian Walter Scheidel, concludes that only mass mobilization wars, transformative revolutions, pandemics or state collapse have redistributed wealth once it has reached current extremes.

Americans have always dreamed that we are an exception to history but we are not. Not only will "incremental change" or the "lesser of two evils" or faith in the wonders of technology fail to prevent disaster—such ideas have delivered us to the crisis we now face. We long for an easy way out—a way that does not demand risk—a way without the only kind of struggle that has ever made history. Of the most likely outcomes that lie ahead transformative revolution and transformative social movements like Standing Rock, are our best chance to minimize violence, reduce harm and create a better world.

Corporate Power is so destructive to democracy and dangerous to the planet because it recognizes no limits other than those imposed upon it. Corporate Power has but one reason for being: the maximum possible profit and the maximum possible power. Corporations must grow or die but now their growth threatens ecocide, perpetual war and the death of democracy. Such a way of life cannot be sustained. There are but few possible outcomes: the internal contradictions of system will drive us to desperate crisis, or we intervene first, rebuild democracy, protect the planet, and overthrow the corporate dictatorship.

Notes

[1]. The 2010 Academy Award winning film Inside Job documents the rise of the corporate state in the context of the 2008 crisis.

VIEWPOINT 5

Democracy Is Good for Business

Freedom House

After several viewpoints arguing that big business is bad for democracy, we now turn to one that says big business has no incentive to support repressive regimes. In the following viewpoint authors from Freedom House argue that fostering democracy is in the interest of businesses. Democracies, the author argues, would be wise to encourage the development and support of strong democratic institutions in their trading partners. Freedom House is an independent watchdog organization dedicated to the expansion of freedom and democracy around the world.

As you read, consider the following questions:

1. Why should established democracies encourage democratic institutions in other countries?
2. What are some of the exceptions to the general principle that democracies have stronger economies?
3. Why are "soft" values important, according to the viewpoint?

Recent diplomatic breakthroughs involving Iran and Cuba could pave the way for major investment by U.S. companies. But despite the excitement generated when an isolated and repressive regime begins to open up its market, an open political system would be much better for business.

"Democracy Is Good for Business," Freedom House, August 3, 2015. Reprinted by permission.

Stable, transparent governments built on respect for human rights and the rule of law tend to foster environments that are conducive to the establishment and unfettered operation of private enterprises. This is clearly illustrated in the World Bank's *Doing Business* survey and Freedom House's *Freedom in the World* report: On average, countries that perform well in one assessment also excel in the other.

Conversely, regimes that oppress their populations are more likely to limit business opportunities. According to *Doing Business*, governments in countries identified as Not Free in *Freedom in the World* generally impose more red tape, build up barriers to trade, and fail to enforce contracts.

The correlation suggests that established democracies could serve their own economic interests by encouraging democratic institutions abroad and thereby improving the business environment over the long term.

Image and Reality

Strong growth in certain repressive systems, especially China, has given the misleading impression that authoritarianism is good for business. The casual observer might see ruthlessly implemented development projects and probusiness legal window dressing as more important to the operating environment than things like parliamentary oversight and freedom of assembly.

However, only a handful of Not Free countries score highly on the *Doing Business* "distance to frontier" measurement, which compares economies as they are with regulatory best practice. Most Not Free states breed corruption due to their opacity and concentration of power, are prone to sudden and arbitrary decisions due to the lack of checks and balances, and are more susceptible to political unrest than democracies because they do not allow peaceful changes of government through elections. None of these traits are helpful to businesses.

A number of developing countries that are often praised for macroeconomic expansion, such as Angola, Ethiopia, and

Uganda, actually receive rather low scores on *Doing Business*, and are rated Not Free by Freedom House for their repression of political opposition and other democratic shortcomings. China earns only a middling score from the World Bank report. While its sheer size and momentum have allowed it to attract massive investment on its own difficult terms, last month's stock-market plunge may have a sobering effect. Myanmar, which has been hailed as a hot investment opportunity since U.S. and European sanctions were lifted, ranks near the bottom of *Doing Business* and continues to imprison journalists and allow persecution of ethnic minorities. Multinational corporations are similarly eager to enter Iran once it is relieved of international sanctions under the recent nuclear agreement, but it too scores poorly on both its regulatory environment and its political rights and civil liberties.

At the positive end of the spectrum, the major democracies of South America, Europe (including newer democracies in the east), East Asia, and South Africa all promote regulatory systems that are as open as their political systems. Even Greece, despite its current struggle with excessive public debt, continues to be rated Free by Freedom House and ranks in the top third of the World Bank's report.

Exceptions and Outliers

There are a number of governments that buck the trend, either combining political freedom and a poor business climate or managing to encourage business while simultaneously clamping down on political rights and civil liberties. Most in the latter camp are small states with the will, incentives, and sufficiently tight control to maintain these clashing priorities. Such governments also tend to treat foreigners and natives differently, welcoming multinational companies and expatriate professionals out of necessity, even as they dominate many aspects of their own citizens' lives. (Low-skilled foreign workers, of course, receive the worst treatment of all.)

Examples include Singapore as well as the Persian Gulf monarchies of Bahrain, Qatar, and the United Arab Emirates.

Rwanda also scores high on *Doing Business* under President Paul Kagame's strong-arm rule; Kagame has made impressive strides against corruption and pushed through other business-friendly measures, but has chosen not to allow parallel improvements in civic and political affairs.

There are also significant democracies that have failed to foster bureaucratic efficiency and predictable conditions in which businesses can thrive. Freedom House has ranked India as Free for nearly 20 years, but the World Bank places it near the bottom on indicators such as the time required to start a business, taxes, and enforcement of contracts. Some African countries that stand out for upholding political rights and civil liberties, such as Benin and Senegal, likewise rate poorly for their business environments.

Democracy is clearly not the only factor behind good economic performance, but more often than not, it provides the long-term political stability and corrective mechanisms that form a foundation for safe investment and steady growth.

Policy Implications

Policymakers often argue that "soft" values such as human rights and democracy must take a backseat to economic and security interests. In a recent report, *Supporting Democracy Abroad*, Freedom House found that even top-performing Sweden failed to consistently promote democracy and human rights in its trade policy.

Such prioritization is shortsighted. A more democratic world would be a more stable, inviting place for established democracies to trade and invest. The political crackdowns and security crises associated with authoritarian rule often drive out business and place employees, supply chains, and investments at risk, in addition to raising reputational and legal concerns for foreign companies that stay involved.

Therefore, democratic governments seeking to bolster the global economy and develop new markets should press their counterparts not just for lower barriers to trade and less red tape, but also for strong and accountable democratic institutions.

Periodical and Internet Sources Bibliography

The following articles have been selected to supplement the diverse views presented in this chapter.

Alexander Blum. "Many Think Capitalism and Democracy Go Together. What if They Don't?" Arc, April 25, 2018. https://arcdigital.media/many-think-capitalism-and-democracy-go-together-what-if-they-dont-3fb9e68b16d1

David Cole, "Artificial Persons: The Long Road to Citizens United," *Nation*, June 6, 2018. https://www.thenation.com/article/artificial-persons/

Russell Dawn, "Why Converting the United States to a Full Democracy Will Only Increase Tyranny," *Federalist*, August 13, 2018. https://thefederalist.com/2018/08/13/why-converting-the-united-states-to-a-democracy-will-increase-tyranny/

Theodore Kupfer, "Democracy Is Surviving *Citizens United*," *National Review*, July 18, 2016. https://www.nationalreview.com/2016/07/citizens-united-2016-campaign-financing-bernie-sanders-donald-trump-jeb-bush/

Michel Rose, "In Athens, Macron to Urge Renewal of EU Democracy," Business Insider, September 5, 2017. http://static3.businessinsider.com/r-in-athens-macron-to-urge-renewal-of-eu-democracy-2017-9

Matt Stoller, "The Return of Monopoly," *New Republic*, July 13, 2017. https://newrepublic.com/article/143595/return-monopoly-amazon-rise-business-tycoon-white-house-democrats-return-party-trust-busting-roots

Astra Taylor, "Time's Up for Capitalism: What Comes Next?" *Nation*, May 6, 2019. https://www.thenation.com/article/democracy-environment-astra-taylor/

Adam Winkler, "'Corporations Are People' Is Built on an Incredible 19th-Century Lie," *Atlantic*, March 5, 2018. https://www.theatlantic.com/business/archive/2018/03/corporations-people-adam-winkler/554852/

CHAPTER 4

The Future of a World Dominated by Global Corporations

VIEWPOINT 1

Just 90 Companies Caused Two-Thirds of Man-Made Global Warming Emissions

Suzanne Goldenberg

The most serious crisis the world will face in the 21st century is global warming. In the following viewpoint Suzanne Goldenberg argues that crisis has been caused, in large part, by just 90 companies. Multinational corporations, not governments, says the author, have created this crisis and they, not governments, should be held responsible. Suzanne Goldenberg is an author and journalist specializing in environmental reporting.

As you read, consider the following questions:

1. What is the "carbon budget" mentioned here and what is the danger of exhausting it?
2. What type of companies were the majority of those in the top 90 emitters discussed in this viewpoint?
3. Who are the big spenders behind climate denial propaganda, according to this viewpoint?

The climate crisis of the 21st century has been caused largely by just 90 companies, which between them produced nearly

---

"Just 90 Companies Caused Two-Thirds of Man-Made Global Warming Emissions," by Suzanne Goldenberg, Guardian News and Media Limited, November 20, 2013. Reprinted by permission.

two-thirds of the greenhouse gas emissions generated since the dawning of the industrial age, new research suggests.

The companies range from investor-owned firms—household names such as Chevron, Exxon and BP—to state-owned and government-run firms.

The analysis, which was welcomed by the former vice-president Al Gore as a "crucial step forward" found that the vast majority of the firms were in the business of producing oil, gas or coal, found the analysis, which has been published in the journal Climatic Change.

"There are thousands of oil, gas and coal producers in the world," climate researcher and author Richard Heede at the Climate Accountability Institute in Colorado said. "But the decision makers, the CEOs, or the ministers of coal and oil if you narrow it down to just one person, they could all fit on a Greyhound bus or two."

Half of the estimated emissions were produced just in the past 25 years—well past the date when governments and corporations became aware that rising greenhouse gas emissions from the burning of coal and oil were causing dangerous climate change.

Many of the same companies are also sitting on substantial reserves of fossil fuel which—if they are burned—puts the world at even greater risk of dangerous climate change.

Climate change experts said the data set was the most ambitious effort so far to hold individual carbon producers, rather than governments, to account.

The United Nations climate change panel, the IPCC, warned in September that at current rates the world stood within 30 years of exhausting its "carbon budget"—the amount of carbon dioxide it could emit without going into the danger zone above 2C warming. The former US vice-president and environmental champion, Al Gore, said the new carbon accounting could re-set the debate about allocating blame for the climate crisis.

Leaders meeting in Warsaw for the UN climate talks this week clashed repeatedly over which countries bore the burden for solving the climate crisis—historic emitters such as America or Europe or the rising economies of India and China.

Gore in his comments said the analysis underlined that it should not fall to governments alone to act on climate change.

"This study is a crucial step forward in our understanding of the evolution of the climate crisis. The public and private sectors alike must do what is necessary to stop global warming," Gore told the Guardian. "Those who are historically responsible for polluting our atmosphere have a clear obligation to be part of the solution."

Between them, the 90 companies on the list of top emitters produced 63% of the cumulative global emissions of industrial carbon dioxide and methane between 1751 to 2010, amounting to about 914 gigatonne CO_2 emissions, according to the research. All but seven of the 90 were energy companies producing oil, gas and coal. The remaining seven were cement manufacturers.

The list of 90 companies included 50 investor-owned firms—mainly oil companies with widely recognised names such as Chevron, Exxon, BP, and Royal Dutch Shell and coal producers such as British Coal Corp, Peabody Energy and BHP Billiton.

Some 31 of the companies that made the list were state-owned companies such as Saudi Arabia's Saudi Aramco, Russia's Gazprom and Norway's Statoil.

Nine were government run industries, producing mainly coal in countries such as China, the former Soviet Union, North Korea and Poland, the host of this week's talks.

Experts familiar with Heede's research and the politics of climate change said they hoped the analysis could help break the deadlock in international climate talks.

"It seemed like maybe this could break the logjam," said Naomi Oreskes, professor of the history of science at Harvard. "There are all kinds of countries that have produced a tremendous amount of historical emissions that we do not normally talk about. We do not normally talk about Mexico or Poland or Venezuela. So then it's not just rich v poor, it is also producers v consumers, and resource rich v resource poor."

Michael Mann, the climate scientist, said he hoped the list would bring greater scrutiny to oil and coal companies' deployment of their remaining reserves. "What I think could be a game changer here is the potential for clearly fingerprinting the sources of those future emissions," he said. "It increases the accountability for fossil fuel burning. You can't burn fossil fuels without the rest of the world knowing about it."

Others were less optimistic that a more comprehensive accounting of the sources of greenhouse gas emissions would make it easier to achieve the emissions reductions needed to avoid catastrophic climate change.

John Ashton, who served as UK's chief climate change negotiator for six years, suggested that the findings reaffirmed the central role of fossil fuel producing entities in the economy.

"The challenge we face is to move in the space of not much more than a generation from a carbon-intensive energy system to a carbonneutral energy system. If we don't do that we stand no chance of keeping climate change within the 2C threshold," Ashton said.

"By highlighting the way in which a relatively small number of large companies are at the heart of the current carbon-intensive growth model, this report highlights that fundamental challenge."

Meanwhile, Oreskes, who has written extensively about corporate-funded climate denial, noted that several of the top companies on the list had funded the climate denial movement.

"For me one of the most interesting things to think about was the overlap of large scale producers and the funding of disinformation campaigns, and how that has delayed action," she said.

The data represents eight years of exhaustive research into carbon emissions over time, as well as the ownership history of the major emitters.

The companies' operations spanned the globe, with company headquarters in 43 different countries. "These entities extract resources from every oil, natural gas and coal province in the world, and process the fuels into marketable products that are sold to consumers on every nation on Earth," Heede writes in the paper.

The largest of the investor-owned companies were responsible for an outsized share of emissions. Nearly 30% of emissions were produced just by the top 20 companies, the research found.

By Heede's calculation, government-run oil and coal companies in the former Soviet Union produced more greenhouse gas emissions than any other entity—just under 8.9% of the total produced over time. China came a close second with its government-run entities accounting for 8.6% of total global emissions.

ChevronTexaco was the leading emitter among investor-owned companies, causing 3.5% of greenhouse gas emissions to date, with Exxon not far behind at 3.2%. In third place, BP caused 2.5% of global emissions to date.

The historic emissions record was constructed using public records and data from the US department of energy's Carbon Dioxide Information and Analysis Centre, and took account of emissions all along the supply chain.

The centre put global industrial emissions since 1751 at 1,450 gigatonnes.

VIEWPOINT 2

After Paris, Businesses Not Governments Are Leading the Climate Change Fight

Daphne Leprince-Ringuet

In the previous viewpoint, the author discussed how just 90 corporations are responsible for the vast majority of environmental damage and have little incentive to change their ways. In the following viewpoint Daphne Leprince-Ringuet explores the trend of corporations stepping up to lead the fight against climate change and points out that due to the imperative for swift action on climate change, corporations may be in a much better position than governments are to actually make a difference. Daphne Leprince-Ringuet is a writer and journalist and frequent contributor to Wired UK.

As you read, consider the following questions:

1. Why is it more difficult for governments to take quick action than for corporations, according to the author?
2. Why does the transition to more environmentally-friendly industry require so much investment,?
3. What, according to the viewpoint, was the response of multinationals such as Apple and Tesla to the Trump administration's withdrawal from the Paris Climate Agreement?

"Businesses Not Governments Are Leading the Climate Change Fight," by Daphne Leprince-Ringuet, Condé Nast, December 20, 2018. Reprinted by permission.

For two weeks at the start of December, the United Nations met to create the "Paris Rulebook" for fighting climate change. Although they eventually agreed a plan, scientists are still sceptical that it will be enough to keep carbon pollution to safe levels.

But it is not all doom and gloom. While delegates were debating, Denmark-based shipping company Maersk, which is the largest in the industry, announced its own plans to cut its net carbon emissions to zero by 2050. The move received much less media coverage. But the industry accounts for more than two per cent of global carbon emissions.

So are businesses moving faster than politicians? Maersk's announcement seems reflective of such a trend. For David Wei, director for climate at sustainable consultancy firm Business for Social Responsibility (BSR), the COP24 meeting did send a positive signal to businesses—concluding a common rule book, in today's global political scene, is no small feat. "Just because we set the rules of the road doesn't mean we will be driving faster," he says. "And in this case, the success lies in driving faster."

But while politicians discuss and negotiate those rules, businesses are actually stepping up. At the end of November, just before the start of the COP24, 50 major global businesses from the World Economic Forum representing $1.5 trillion in revenue (£1.19 trillion) signed an open letter calling for stronger action at COP24.

Thirty of the signatories have already succeeded in reducing emissions by nine per cent between 2015 and 2016—that's the equivalent of taking 10 million cars off the road for a year. And all of the businesses that signed agreed to urge governments to fast-track solutions to tackle climate change. The letter offered three ideas to ponder on at the talks: implementing better carbon-pricing mechanisms, providing incentive for low-carbon investments and improving education to encourage societies to shift away from high-carbon solutions.

And days before the COP24 started, British business magnate Richard Branson, the founder of the Virgin Group, said: "I'm glad businesses are committed to taking action now—it's absurd to think governments wouldn't do the same."

But are they—or at least, are they taking action enough to match businesses' expectations? For Katrien Steenmans, researcher in environmental law at the University of Surrey, the outcome of the latest COP shows that they are not. "With some of the key decisions postponed until COP25 and beyond," she says, "governments are neither delivering faster change nor clearer signals as demanded by leading organisations from the World Economic Forum in November."

In the context of the time-critical nature of climate change, she describes the progress made in the last two weeks as "weak" and "inadequate". And indeed, there seems to be a gap between policy-makers and industries. Opening his talk on climate finance in the second week of the COP24, Michael Eckhart, the managing director of the American investment bank Citigroup, said: "Am I the only commercial banker in this room? We need half this room to be filled with financiers."

It would be incorrect, however, to claim that nothing was done. A total of over £100 million was pledged overall to be allocated to the Adaptation Fund, to help developing countries adapt to climate change; as well as over £8 billion to be contributed to the Green Climate Fund, which encourages investment in low-emission development. And the proposal drafted by Michal Kurtyka, the designated president of this year's COP, highlights the urgent need to scale up climate finance through private and public resources.

"This is crucial because we are talking about an unprecedented global transition that requires equally massive financial input," says Megan Bowman, co-author of a study on climate finance law and associate professor at King's College in London. "There is a multi-trillion dollar gap between where we are now and where we need to be for a low-carbon and more resilient world." To bridge this gap, she continues, efforts should come from national law-makers as much as corporations. "It's all hands on deck," she says.

But when it comes to making change happen, it seems that private businesses have been a lot more proactive. Last week, while the COP24 was underway, more than 400 global investors with more than $30 trillion (£23.82 trillion) in assets called on global leaders to increase climate action, including demands to phase out coal. Meanwhile, Volkswagen announced that its next generation of combustion cars would be the last. A total of 43 fashion brands including Burberry and Adidas launched the Fashion Industry Charter for Climate Action, to address the impact of the fashion sector across its entire value chain.

In the UK, BT's strategy to integrate renewable electricity in its supply chain was used by non-profit organisation The Climate Group as a guide for other companies to follow. The telecommunications giant has announced its goal of using 100 per cent renewable electricity by 2020, and to reduce its carbon emission intensity by 87 per cent compared to the levels it recorded in the last year. It has also started adding an "emission reduction clause" to contracts with its network suppliers, like Huawei for instance, requiring them to reduce their carbon emissions over the duration of the contract.

Gabrielle Giner, the head of environmental sustainability at BT, is far from dismissing progress made at the COP. The common rule book, she says, will drive climate action. "That said," she continues, "we need our policymakers to continue to set more ambitious targets, which will focus the minds of both business and government, allowing for deeper and faster action."

For David Wei, deeper and faster action will be exactly the focus of next year's COP and what, according to him, "everyone will be watching for". We are reaching a point where establishing rules is a positive step, albeit one that has to be followed with the scaling up of ambition. Something that some businesses have already put their head to.

Political turmoil may have grabbed a few headlines at the COP24, therefore, but in the meantime real action is already happening at the heart of industries. This is particularly true across the pond. As soon as US President Donald Trump announced that he would back out of the Paris Agreement last year, companies including Apple, Tesla or Facebook were quick to clarify that they would remain on the low-carbon bandwagon.

Businesses are yet to react to the outcome of the COP24. "It is a massive letdown that governments have not risen to the challenge of delivering faster change at COP24, but this should not stop others from taking action," says Steenmans.

VIEWPOINT 3

Corporations Need a New Strategy for Responding to Climate Change

Rory Sullivan

In the following viewpoint Rory Sullivan acknowledges that many businesses are aiming to limit emissions of greenhouse gases but points out that there is more they could and should do. Businesses are, the author says, still focusing on relatively low-risk, low-cost actions. He argues that they should respond to the risks of climate change as they would to other long-term risks that face their businesses. Rory Sullivan is an internationally recognized expert on the financial and investment implications of climate change. He has written several books on finance, climate change, and corporate responsibility.

As you read, consider the following questions:

1. What are businesses doing wrong in their response to climate change, according to the author?
2. How, according to this viewpoint, might businesses see climate change as an opportunity as well as a risk?
3. Why does the probabilistic nature of climate change science make it more difficult for corporations to respond to it, and how does the author suggest companies deal with this?

"Climate Change Strategy for Business," by Rory Sullivan, Guardian News and Media Limited, July 22, 2011. Reprinted by permission.

Most large companies now see managing their greenhouse gas emissions and minimising energy consumption as integral parts of their environmental management practices. Many have set targets to reduce their greenhouse gas emissions, have worked with their suppliers and customers to reduce their emissions, and have encouraged governments to adopt policies directed at significantly reducing global greenhouse gas emissions.

Yet, climate change remains an issue that is primarily seen as one of operational efficiency rather than the creation of long term sustainable value. The majority of companies have focused their efforts on those actions that provide clear and relatively low risk returns, and those where the costs are relatively modest. This wait and see approach, perhaps unsurprisingly, is particularly prevalent in situations where the actions involve significant capital expenditures (eg in the power generation sector) or where the actions could commit the company irrevocably to a specific course of action (eg discontinuing a particular product line).

When challenged, companies cite the huge uncertainties in climate change policy at the national and international levels as the major barrier to them thinking about climate change in any terms other than relatively short term costs and benefits. While there is a logic in this line of argument, it is striking that climate change, in many ways (eg pervasive uncertainty, major implications for huge swathes of the economy, changing public and consumer attitudes), looks exactly the same as many of the other strategic issues that companies need to address. While there may be a concern among business leaders about the risks inherent in responding to—or being seen to respond to—a green issue, the reality is that, from a business perspective, climate change is a long term structural change.

If we frame climate change as a strategic issue, the logical conclusion is that companies should think about climate change-related risks and opportunities in a similar manner to other business risks and opportunities. That is, they should assess how climate change may affect their business and, based on this assessment, make decisions that allows them to protect their business against downside risks, maximise upside opportunities and ensure that their business strategies are not a one way bet on climate change policy (in either direction). Expressed another way, companies need to make decisions that take proper account of uncertainty, that properly account for the longer term trajectory of climate change policy but that are sufficiently robust and flexibility to respond to the inevitable changes in the business, market and policy context in which they work.

What does this look like in practice? First, it suggests that companies need to rethink the time horizons they use in their corporate risk assessment and strategy processes. While most large companies already have structured processes for identifying and assessing the business implications of potential changes in regulation, changes in consumer attitudes, NGO campaigns, etc, most tend to concentrate on short to medium term risks, typically those with a maximum time horizon of three to five years. Because the effects of climate change are both probabilistic and likely to occur over a longer time frame, this three to five year frame of reference is likely to see many important dimensions of climate change-related risk simply excluded from analysis.

Second, it suggests that companies need to revisit their capital investment processes. For most companies, the single biggest opportunity they have to future proof their businesses and create longer term business value is when they invest capital, whether into new projects, new products or upgrading existing equipment. If climate change is factored into these decisions (eg through a shadow price of carbon, through considering a range of scenarios about regulation and the physical impacts of climate change), it maximises the likelihood that companies will make decisions that do not result in stranded assets or lost revenues because of regulatory or other action on climate change, and will avoid the need for extensive retrofits at a later date.

Third, it suggests that companies need to develop corporate information, knowledge and expertise on climate change. The

> ## Anti-Shopping Goes Mainstream
>
> Traditionally, the work of marketers has been to encourage the shopper to buy. For decades, marketers have focused on understanding, segmenting, or empirically dissecting a product or brand's existing customer base to identify and grow the customer base.
>
> But what happens when consumers choose not to shop? Once thought of as on the fringe, consumer resistance movements that eschew consumption are becoming increasingly mainstream. These so-called "inscrutable shoppers" are commonly anti-globalisation, anti-sweatshop, anti-chain store movements, and anti-technology.
>
> Although a challenge, consumer resistance can provide opportunities. For instance, during poor economic conditions, some retailers are driven to develop innovative strategies around offering cash or a trade-in in exchange for unwanted electronics.
>
> During tough economic times, Amazon was able to re-engage consumers in the purchase process by offering gift cards in exchange for second-hand video games. The gift card idea was ingenious as, rather than paying cash for used games, Amazon re-engaged consumers to purchase more from Amazon.com.
>
> Savvy retailers can meet specific challenges, such as consumer boredom. For example, the mall-based family centre KidZania entertains

companies that have gone furthest in integrating climate change into their business strategies emphasise how much time and effort they have invested in testing new technologies and new approaches. This means that when it comes to investment (eg in a new vehicle fleet) they fully understand not only the financial aspects of their decisions (ie the costs and benefits of a specific technology) but also the operational and other implications (eg maintenance of the new equipment, the availability of specific raw materials).

In conclusion, climate change is a strategic issue for companies, and needs to be seen as such. The fact that its origins are in debates around resource consumption and resource depletion make it no less important an issue. The companies that will be best positioned to respond to the inevitable business and societal stresses imposed

> and educates children by immersing them in a simulated city where children role-play as citizens.
>
> T-shirt designers Threadless cater for the consumer who wants to co-create the product; similarly Shoes of Prey allows customers to design and customise their own shoes.
>
> Others have responded in a way that has maintained or increased their customer base. For example, luxury lingerie brand La Perla has embraced the "slow shopping movement" to enhance the customer experience by engaging them in the story of the product during a leisurely online or store visit.
>
> In drawing out the implications for retailers, we propose a number of strategies by which retailers can connect and engage with today's shopper, ranging from the offer of edutainment within the physical store environment, to a holistic strategy of thinking global, acting local.
>
> Other technological advances mean that retailers are increasingly able to connect with and engage consumers across multiple channels, and to involve consumers in the communication and creation to mitigate consumer resistance.
>
> *"The Anti-Shopping Movement Goes Mainstream," by Sean Sands, The Conversation, January 13, 2012.*

by climate change will be those that have recognised climate change as a strategic driver of business value, that have taken a longer term view of the business implications of climate change, and that have built climate change into their capital investment decisions.

Viewpoint 4

It's Not Too Late to Save Democracy from Corporate Greed

Japheth J. Omojuwa

In the following viewpoint, Japheth J. Omojuwa turns back to the issue of global corporate dominance and its effect on democracy, drawing on examples from African nations, Europe, and the United States. Corruption and financial crimes and what the author calls "the corrupting influence of money" have reduced democracy to a sham. However, the future of democracy may not be so grim, this author says, if the people demand transparency and accountability from their leaders. Japheth J. Omojuwa is a Nigerian political commentator, author, and columnist.

As you read, consider the following questions:

1. How does the author sum up what has happened to democracy in the twenty-first century?
2. What is one of the biggest threats to democracy today, according to Omojuwa?
3. What suggestions does he offer for restoring democracy?

In his prime, he was a force to be reckoned with, a phenomenon the world over. No man could defeat him. In the ring, Mike Tyson would pulverize any opponent he came up against—faster and more efficiently than anyone before him.

"Democracy Sold Out to Corruption and Greed. But It's Not Too Late to Save It," by Japheth J. Omojuwa, World Economic Forum, August 19, 2016. Reprinted by permission.

But outside the ring it was a different story. Even as he celebrated victory after victory, he was already on his way down. Tyson was training less, and partying and gambling more. The one thing he didn't do eventually cost him his legacy: he stopped training hard. Long before he lost to Buster Douglas in Japan, he had stopped being Mike Tyson, or at least the Mike Tyson the world had come to know.

Even though its Buster Douglas moment is yet to come, this is the story of democracy in the 21st century. It has been reduced to a mere process whose outcome no longer matters, as long as elections are held. We used to have dictators who came to power by undermining elections. Today we have dictators who are enthroned and legitimized by elections. Democracy has lost its way and its essence.

Turning Our Backs on Democracy

Abraham Lincoln's definition of democracy remains the most intuitive essence of this form of government: government of the people, by the people, for the people.

In many supposed democracies around the world, this has either completely changed, or is changing right before our eyes. And an increasingly disillusioned electorate seems to welcome it.

Voter turn-out is the lowest it has been around the world in a generation. Voters have lost faith in politicians and are turning to demagogues. Donald Trump—and the things he represents—is no outlier.

Just look to the UK, where a populist party helped drag the country out of the European Union, and dragged the global economy down with it. Or look at Austria, where the FPÖ, a party founded by a Nazi functionary, could win the presidential rerun. Or look at France, where the Front National—a party with a well-known racist and anti-Semitic past—grows in popularity by the day. Apart from their appeal to dark politics and hatred, these demagogues all have one thing in common: they have a following we can't pretend doesn't exist.

The people want anything but democracy. And who can blame them when we see what it has become? When in the US, the world's largest democracy, government can push through a trade agreement—the TPP—without so much as consulting people, never mind informing them of its monumental impact. What happened to transparency, to accountability? Is it any wonder voter confidence is falling as fast as turnout?

This Is What Happens When Democracy Sells Out

It's not hard to figure out there's a connection between these two trends. The less we trust our political elite, the more likely we are to take a gamble on one of these demagogues. After all, can a fear-monger be any worse than the cronyism and lies democracy has become?

Democracy was built on the power and needs of the people. It has since sold out to money. And that, experts agree, is the biggest threat to it today.

"This is one of the main reasons leading to disenchanted voters and the rise of populist parties in the United States and the European Union," Daniel Freund, the head of advocacy at Transparency International EU, points out.

If the corruptive influence of money has left voter in the West disenchanted, it has been even more damaging in Africa.

Take Nigeria. Voters there are no longer shocked by revelations of corruption uncovered by the country's anti-graft agency, the Economic and Financial Crimes Commission. Hundreds of millions of dollars have already been seized from politicians and public officials who served under the previous government, and millions—even billions—more remain to be recovered. Citizens are disgruntled and democracy no longer looks as promising as it did in 1999, when the military handed over to a democratically elected president.

It's a similar story over in Zimbabwe. President Robert Mugabe might claim to have popular support, but regular protests against his government suggests otherwise. "The government has stolen our money. It is out of touch with the problems we have. It must begin to listen to the people and stamp out the corruption which has crippled our economy," Pastor Evan Mawarire, the leader of a popular Zimbabwean protest group, told the Guardian last month.

For a long time, oligarchs in the garb of democrats pretended to serve the interests of the people. But the veil of deception is lifting. People are starting to recognize that the dreams of collective prosperity promised by democracy are being turned into nightmares for the majority, and monumental wealth for the privileged ruling class and their allies.

Saving Democracy from Itself

There is a common thread: if it does not look like democracy and does not have the outcomes we would expect from democracy, it is not a democracy.

As Francois de La Rochefoucauld once wrote, we should not trust democracy without extremely powerful systems of accountability. In many so-called democracies today, that accountability—and the transparency that goes with it—is missing. As this trend continues, democracy will continue to appear strong and ready to meet all challenges, but like Mike Tyson discovered in Japan, once an idea loses its essence, it will gradually fade away. What will take its place is a world we do not want to envisage, let alone live in.

But it's not too late. Democracy can still become of the people, by the people and for the people once again, in process and in outcomes, in deed and in truth. Just as Rome was not built in a day, so the Roman Empire did not end when Romulus was overthrown by Odoacer. No, the fall of Rome began long before its rulers saw their world order was on its way out.

Lamia Merzuki is a member of the African Leadership Network. As far as she is concerned, "in many countries, people just don't trust politicians and their ability to change things anymore." To make sure this lack of trust in politicians does not translate into a complete lack of trust in democracy, we must now begin to focus on making transparency and accountability fundamental to our acceptance of a government as democratic.

The same way attending school for a day does not make one a graduate, elections should not determine which countries we recognize as democratic.

Once we accept what it means to be a truly democratic country, we'll have started the journey towards separating democracies from their adulterations all around the world. Let's hope we can do so before democracy fades into but a shadow of its former self.

VIEWPOINT 5

To Reclaim Democracy, Amend the US Constitution

Reclaim the American Dream

In the United States, at least, some of the problems with democracy can be addressed by amending the nation's constitution, according to authors at Reclaim the American Dream in the following excerpted viewpoint. Huge amounts of money from corporations, made legal by the US Supreme Court case known as Citizens United, *have corrupted the political process and reduced the power of individual voters to influence elections, the authors say. Many state and local governments are already calling for reform and this viewpoint outlines their efforts. Reclaim the American Dream is a website dedicated to providing information to Americans interested in fixing their democracy.*

As you read, consider the following questions:

1. What different responses were mounted by states in response to the Citizens United decision, as outlined here?
2. Republican voters seem to support reducing the impact of big money on elections, but Republican leaders are split on the issue. Based on other viewpoints in this volume, why might that be the case?
3. What do the authors mean when they say that the US Congress is out of step with voters?

"Progress Report: Amend the Constitution," Reclaim the American Dream. Reprinted by permission.

Nineteen states from coast to coast, reacting against the Citizens United decision, have gone on record in favor of a U.S. constitutional amendment to restore the power of Congress and the states to put some limits on campaign spending. At the local level, too, there's a crescendo in the call for reform. More than 700 local governments from Sarasota, FL to Midway City, KY and Conway, Arkansas to Salt Lake City, Utah and San Luis Obispo, California have also demanded constitutional action to reinstitute controls on campaign spending.

State actions have come either through popular referendums, legislative resolutions or collective letters from state legislators to Congress. Among cities, the Los Angeles referendum in May 2013 is fairly typical. Passed by a 77% majority vote, it instructed elected officials to press for an amendment,stating that "there should be limits on political campaign spending and that corporations should not have the constitutional rights of human beings."

[…]

The Push for Reform Came Fast

Grass roots reaction came swiftly against the Supreme Court's ruling in January 2010 in Citizens United that authorized unlimited spending by corporations and unions from their general treasuries.

Just three months later, the state legislature in Hawaii passed a resolution calling on Congress to propose and send to the states a Constitutional Amendment restoring to Congress and the states the power to regulate corporate campaign donations.

In 2012, legislatures in Vermont, Massachusetts, New Jersey and California, passed similar resolutions. In 2013, legislative action for a constitutional amendment was taken by Illinois, Maine, New Mexico, Oregon and West Virginia.

As the movement spread, some states took a different approach. In Delaware and Maryland a majority of the state's Senate and House of Delegates signed a letter to Congress calling for a Constitutional amendment. In Connecticut, a majority of the state's senators and representatives signed a similar letter. In New York, majorities of lawmakers in both houses of the state legislature signed five different letters from different party caucuses, all calling for a constitutional amendment to reverse the impact of the *Citizens United* ruling and restore legislative power to regulate campaign finance.

Groundswell from the Grass Roots

But the most striking show of popular discontent and the most visible popular groundswell for campaign reform came in in the November 2012 elections in the states of Colorado and Montana. The votes in those two states demonstrated that at the grass roots, the drive to control the rising tide of Mega Money in elections draws support from across the political spectrum—from Republicans, independents and Democrats.

In Colorado, every single county in the state had a majority in favor of reform—those that are predominantly Republican as well as those dominated by Democrats or counties that are a mix of D's, R;'s and independents. The reform measure was backed by more than 1,650,000 voters, or roughly 73% of the total vote. the margin of victory was similar in Montana.

In the November 2016 elections, ballot initiatives for an anti-Citizens United constitutional amendment won solid majorities in popular vote referendums in California and Washington State.

Congress Is Out of Step with Voters

Even so, Congress still resists what opinion polls show to be the demand of a large majority of voters for reform on campaign finance. In September 2014, a majority of U.S. Senators voted in favor of a constitutional amendment but their 54-42 majority fell short of the 60 votes needed to overcome the threat of an opposition filibuster. It was a partisan clash: All 42 "No" votes came from Republicans and all 54 "Yes" votes came from Democrats.

But solid Republican opposition to systemic reforms is splintering. During the 2016 presidential primary campaign, GOP presidential contenders. Sen. Lindsay Graham of South Carolina, and former Florida Governor Jeb Bush came out in favor of a constitutional amendment. In various states, some Republican legislators support reforms to curb runaway campaign spending as does U.S. Rep. Walter Jones, a North Carolina Tea Party Republican. "If we want to change Washington and return power to the citizens of this nation, we have to change the way campaigns are financed," Jones asserts. "The status quo is dominated by deep-pocketed special interests, and that's simply unacceptable to the American people."

New Hampshire Towns Vote Yes

New Hampshire is typical of states where a constitutional amendment on MoneyPolitics has generated a clash between elected lawmakers and grass roots opinion. New Hampshire still uses traditional town meetings and local petitions to let voters take a stand on issues. Since 2014, voters in 69 towns have passed local ballot initiatives calling for a constitutional amendment to reverse the *Citizens United* decision and to limit campaign spending.

In May 2014, heeding the town votes, a solid majority of the New Hampshire House of Representatives—154 Democrats joined by 29 Republicans—voted in favor of a constitutional amendment resolution. But ten days later, the Republican majority in the state senate voted 12-11 to block the proposal.

In 2015, campaign reform was back on the legislature's agenda, with Republicans controlling both houses. The senate gave unanimous bipartisan approval to a bill "recognizing the need" for a U.S. constitutional amendment and tasking a study committee to analyze the options. But the house did a zig-zag dance. A strong resolution endorsing a constitutional amendment narrowly passed, but minutes later, with the electronic voting machines malfunctioning, that vote was reversed. Vote switching by 13 house Republicans killed the bill, setting up constitutional reform as a campaign issue in 2016.

Taking Voter Protest to the U.S. Capitol Steps

Even with all the popular backing already generated, any effort to amend the U.S. Constitution entails a sustained popular campaign for passage. As polls indicate, so many Americans are angry about skyrocketing campaign spending by corporations and the super rich that the issue keeps gaining momentum around the country.

Average Americans say they don't want to see American democracy on the auction block, sold to the highest bidder. Popular grass roots pressures have caused hundreds of city councils, county commissions and state legislators to endorse a constitutional amendment.

In April 2016, several thousand Americans took a week of protest marches to the U.S. Capitol steps to underscore public anger at Congress for ignoring popular demands for constitutional reforms to restore controls on campaign spending. In an echo of the civil rights protests of the 1960s, demonstrators who came from as far away as Guam and Presque Isle, Maine and some of whom marched by foot 140 miles from Philadelphia, engaged in civil disobedience, deliberately inviting arrest to try to force Congress to take notice.

In all, 1,300 people were arrested, including such leaders as Kai Newkirk of 99Rise, Robert Weissman of Public Citizen, Larry Cohen, former president of the Communications Workers of America, Cornell Brooks of the NAACP, Rev. William Barber, leader of North Carolina's Moral Monday movement, and Ben Cohen and Jerry Greenfield of Ben & Jerry's ice cream. Several thousands more marchers and activists cheered those who dared arrest.

"I believe that courage is contagious," said demonstrator Frances Moore Lappe of Boston."If other people see us taking action, then I think they'll have the courage to join in." Newkirk said it was crucial to move beyond emails and tweeting to direct action to show politicians how strongly Americans feel about the money corrupting our democracy. Weissman asserted that the protest week organized by the Democracy Spring and Democracy

Awakening signaled that the reform movement is stepping up its militancy.

A Legal Move to Undercut SuperPAC Funding

Three months later, in July, a bipartisan group of six members and candidates for Congress made a direct challenge to the funding of SuperPACs in a formal complaint to the Federal Election Commission. With a high profile bipartisan legal team drawn from Harvard and the Bush Administration, they argued that the D.C. Circuit Court of Appeals, in the SpeechNow.org case, had stretched the Supreme Court's Citizens United decision in a way that left a ceiling on contributions to candidates but no limits on funding for SuperPACs.

"The situation … is one that Congress never enacted and people would never support," said Laurence Tribe, professor of constitutional law at Harvard. "The law permits a very severe limit on the amount an individual can give to someone's campaign, but at the same time that could be evaded by giving millions to SuperPACs….The Supreme Court never approved anything like that."

But with the FEC paralyzed for years by a three-to-three Republican-Democratic split, analysts were dubious about the prospects for the complaint. In a comment to *The Washington Post*, conservative election law attorney James Bopp Jr. dismissed it as "a case going nowhere."

Periodical and Internet Sources Bibliography

The following articles have been selected to supplement the diverse views presented in this chapter.

Max Boot, "Democracy Is in Crisis around the World. Why?" *Washington Post*, November 21, 2018. https://www.washingtonpost.com/opinions/global-opinions/democracy-is-in-crisis-around-the-world-why/2018/11/21/ccb6423c-ecf4-11e8-8679-934a2b33be52_story.html?utm_term=.70d2fef13dd3

Geoffrey Gertz, "The Future of Capitalism in Emerging Markets," Brookings, February 7, 2019. https://www.brookings.edu/blog/future-development/2019/02/07/the-future-of-capitalism-in-emerging-markets/

Brian Grodsky, "Russia, Putin Lead the Way in Exploiting Democracy's Lost Promise," Conversation, May 22, 2018. https://theconversation.com/russia-putin-lead-the-way-in-exploiting-democracys-lost-promise-94798

Greg Ip, "Two Capitalists Worry about Capitalism's Future," *Wall Street Journal*, April 24, 2019. https://www.wsj.com/articles/two-capitalists-worry-about-capitalisms-future-11556110982

Leighanne Levensaler, "How Tomorrow's Leaders Will Survive the Storm," *Forbes*, July 14, 2016. https://www.forbes.com/sites/workday/2016/07/14/how-tomorrows-leaders-will-survive-the-storm/#6e3643892c53

Raghuram Rajan, "Big Business Is under Attack—and That's Just What Capitalism Needs to Stay Vibrant," Marketwatch, May 7, 2019. https://www.marketwatch.com/story/big-business-is-under-attack-and-thats-just-what-capitalism-needs-to-stay-vibrant-2019-05-062019

John Paul Rollert, "How Sociopathic Capitalism Came to Rule the World," *Atlantic*, November 2, 2016. https://www.theatlantic.com/business/archive/2016/11/sociopathic-capitalism/506240/

For Further Discussion

Chapter 1
1. What are some advantages to giving corporations rights that individuals do not have?
2. Will China's investment in Africa benefit African nations or just engage in more colonialism? Why?

Chapter 2
1. What specific steps can global corporations take to make their businesses more environmentally sustainable? Do you think these are just token gestures or truly helpful policies?
2. How can corporate control corrupt the media and endanger a free press, and thus democracy?

Chapter 3
1. What is corporate capture of government? Can you think of ways citizens might regain control of their governments?
2. Do you believe that the corporate takeover of western democracy is a done deal? Why or why not?

Chapter 4
1. A few global corporations are responsible for the bulk of emissions contributing to climate change. Do you think these companies can be trusted to address the problem themselves or will an adequate response to the crisis require the intervention of governments?
2. Many people believe that the Supreme Court decision known as *Citizens United* is dangerous to democracy. Do you agree? Support your answer with information about corporate power that you've read in all four chapters of this volume.

Organizations to Contact

The editors have compiled the following list of organizations concerned with the issues debated in this book. The descriptions are derived from materials provided by the organizations. All have publications or information available for interested readers. The list was compiled on the date of publication of the present volume; the information provided here may change. Be aware that many organizations take several weeks or longer to respond to inquiries, so allow as much time as possible.

American Economic Association
2014 Broadway Suite 305
Nashville, TN 37203
(615) 322-2595
email: Contact via web form
website: www.aeaweb.org

The American Economic Association is an organization dedicated to supporting economic research and education. It takes no partisan positions on the issues it covers.

Canadian Economics Association
55 Metcalfe Street, Suite 1300
c/o Fasken Martineau LLP
Ottawa, ON, K1P 6L5
website: www.Economics.ca

This organization is dedicated to advancing economic education through study and research.

Constitution Center
Independence Mall
525 Arch Street
Philadelphia, PA 19106
(215) 409-6600
email: education@constitutioncenter.org
website: wwwconstitutioncenter.org

The Constitution Center is an institution established by the US Congress to spread non-partisan information about the US Constitution, this group has tons of information and many learning activities related to the US government. Readers can find information here about the court cases mentioned in the text.

Corporate Accountability
(617) 695-2525
email: Contact via web site
website: www.corporateaccountability.org

This organization works to stop transnation organizations from devastating democracy, the environment, and human rights and create a world where corporations answer to people, not the other way around.

Global Affairs Canada
125 Sussex Drive
Ottawa, ON
Canada K1A 0G2
website: www.International.gc. ca

Global Affairs Canada is responsible for managing Canada's diplomatic relations. The organization also promotes international trade.

Law and Economics Center of George Mason University, Antonin Scalia Law School

3301 Fairfax Drive
Hazel Hall, Suite 440
Arlington, VA 22201
(703) 993.8040
email: LEC@gmu.edu
website: www.Masonlec.org

The LEC is a leading academic center for the study and research of economics and law. Many of their articles and educational pieces are accessible for non-experts.

Move to Amend

PO Box 188617
Sacramento, CA 95818
(916) 318-8040
email: Contact via web form
website: Movetoamend.org

With its slogan "End corporate rule. Legalize democracy," Move to Amend states its aim of amending the US Constitution to clearly state that money is not speech, and to restore the rights of citizens.

Occupy Wall Street

website: Occupywallst.org

Occupy Wall Street is a leaderless citizen movement, active in 1,500 cities around the world. It is dedicated to reclaiming democracy from large banks and multinational corporations.

Transparency International

Alt-Moabit 96
10559 Berlin
Germany
49-30-3438-200
email: Ti@transparency.org
website: www.Transparency.org

Transparency International works with governments, businesses, and individuals to end corruption, bribery, and secret deals.

World Trade Organization
Centre William Rappard
Rue de Lausanne, 154
Case postale
1211 Genève 2
Switzerland
+41 (0)22 739 51 11
email: enquiries@wto.org
website: www.wto.org

The World Trade Organization deals with the rules of trade among nations. It is an organization of world governments that works to ensure that trade flows smoothly and as freely as possible between nations.

Bibliography of Books

Bremmer, Ian. *Us vs. Them: The Failure of Globalism*. New York, NY: Penguin, 2018.

Chomsky, Noam. *Who Rules the World?* New York, NY: Henry Hold, 2016.

Ciafone, Amanda. *Counter-Cola: A Multinational History of the Global Corporation*. Oakland, CA: University of California Press, 2019.

Domhoff, G. William. *Who Rules America? The Triumph of the Corporate Rich*. New York, NY: McGraw Hill Education, 2014.

Gitlin, Todd. *Occupy Nation: The Roots, The Spirit, and the Promise of Occupy Wall Street*. New York, NY: It Books/Harper Collins, 2012.

Oreskes , Naomi and Erik M. Conway, *Merchants of Doubt: How a Handful of Scientists Obscured the Truth on Issues from Tobacco Smoke to Global Warming*. New York, NY: Bloomsbury, 2010.

Piketty, Thomas. *Capital in the Twenty-First Century*. Cambridge, MA: Belknap, 2010.

Robert B. Reich. *Saving Capitalism: For the Many, Not the Few*. New York, NY: Knopf, 2015.

Robins, Nick. *The Corporation that Changed the World: How the East India Company Shaped the Modern Multinational*. London, UK: Pluto Press, 2012.

Rodrik, Dani. *The Globalization Paradox: Democracy and the Future of the World Economy*. New York, NY: Norton, 2011.

Steger, Manford B. *Globalization: A Very Short Introduction*. Oxford, UK: Oxford University Press, 2017.

Winkler, Adam. *We the Corporations: How American Businesses Won their Civil Rights*. New York, NY: Liveright, 2018.

Index

A

Africa, colonial history of, 19–28
American Revolution, 15
Anderson, Sarah, 91–96
anti-shopping movement, 154–155

B

Babic, Milan, 76–79
Belt and Road Initiative, 33, 35, 36, 37
Berger, Nahuel, 64–65
Brazil, corporate influence on politics in, 46–50

C

carbon budget, explanation of, 141, 142
carbon dioxide emissions, increase in caused by globalization, 60, 142, 143, 145
Caro, David, 29, 31
Cavanagh, John, 91–96
China, investment in Africa, 33–38, 39–45
climate change, 16, 32, 60, 82, 141–145, 146–150, 151–155

commodity dependence, 39, 44
Communications Act (1934), 87
corporate capture, explanation of, 112–118
corporate consolidation, concentration of by nation, 141–145
corporate media, effect of on politics, 80–90
corporations, history of, 14–16, 19–28

D

democracy, history of corporate influence on, 112–118, 119–127, 128–134, 135–138, 156–160, 161–166

E

East India Company, 15
Ellis-Petersen, Hannah, 124–125
EurActive, 29–32

F

Facebook, and Rohingya crisis, 124–125
Fichtner, Jan, 76–79

Frankema, Ewout, 39–45
Freedom House, 135–138

G

Gleeson, Patrick, 24–25
global apartheid, 91, 94
globalization, criticisms of, 59–68, 76–79, 91–96
Goldenberg, Suzanne, 141–145
government, history of corporate influence on, 105–111

H

Hankla, Charles, 51–56
hate speech, and corporate media, 124–125
Hayes, Rutherford B., 15
health care industry, corporate social responsibility in, 74–75
Heemskerk, Eelke, 76–79

K

Kennedy, Liz, 112–118
Kyoto protocol, 60

L

Lamoreaux, Naomi, 120, 123–126
Leprince-Ringuet, Daphne, 146–150

Lincoln, Abraham, 19, 20–21, 157
Lula da Silva, Luiz Inácio, 46–50

M

Mazzucato, Mariana, 110
Meade, William, 97–102
Moser, Richard, 128–134
multinational companies, characteristics of, 24–25, 69–75
Myanmar, 124–125

N

new colonialism, 33, 37
New Hampshire, and proposed constitutional amendment, 164
Novak, William, 120, 123–126
Nye, Joseph, 105, 106–107, 109, 111

O

oil prices, increase in caused by globalization, 61–62
Omojuwa, Japheth J., 156–160

P

parent company liability lawsuits, 97–102
Paris Climate Agreement, 146–150

Q

quantitative easing, 66, 67

R

Rahman, K. Sabeel, 119–127
Reclaim the American Dream, 161–166
repressive regimes, corporate influence as hindrance to, 135–138
Rohingya crisis, 124–125

S

Sands, Sean, 154–155
Shah, Anup, 19–28
slavery, 21, 26, 34, 39–42, 122
small businesses, regulation of, 29–32
Smith, Adam, 21, 27–28
Smith, David, 105–111
social responsibility, and multinational corporations, 69–75
Street, Paul, 7, 80–90
Sullivan, Rory, 151–155

T

Tanzania, Chinese investment in, 33–38
tariffs, on Chinese goods in the United States, 51–56
Tazara railway line, 36–37
trade war, between China and United States, 51–56
Tverberg, Gail, 59–68

U

United Kingdom, environmental and human rights lawsuits in, 97–102
United States, influence of corporations on politics in, 15–16, 22, 80–90, 161–166
US Constitution, proposed amendment to, 161–166

V

Van Mead, Nick, 33–38
Virginia Company, 15

W

Wharton School of the University of Pennsylvania, 69–75
Winkler, Adam, 120–123, 124, 125

Y

Younge, Gary, 46–50